A Crabby Book

School's In, Crabby!

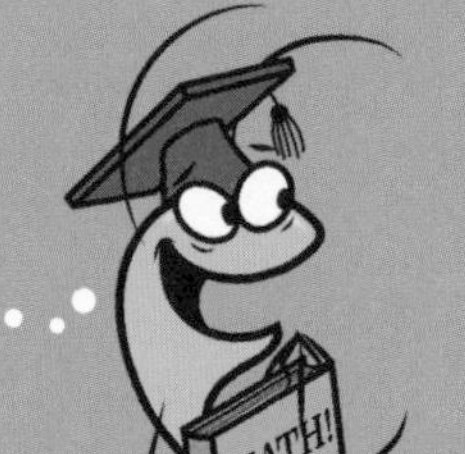
MATH!

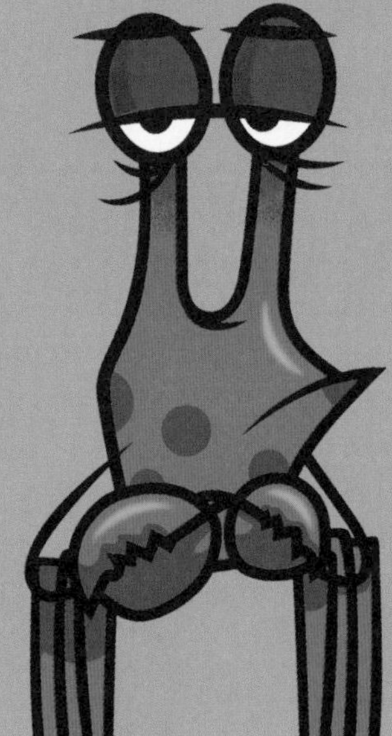

Jonathan Fenske

ACORN™
SCHOLASTIC INC.

For Ms. Sutherland and Ms. Oravetz,
whose kindness made school a joy!

Library of Congress Cataloging-in-Publication Data

Names: Fenske, Jonathan, author, illustrator.
Title: School's in, Crabby! / Jonathan Fenske.
Description: First edition. | New York : Acorn/Scholastic Inc., 2022. | Series: A Crabby book ; 5 |
Summary: Plankton gets the idea to play school with Crabby as the student, but Crabby is more interested in recess and uses wordplay to confuse Plankton and get his way.
Identifiers: LCCN 2021051269 (print) | ISBN 9781338756500 (hardcover) |
ISBN 9781338756494 (paperback)
Subjects: LCSH: Crabs—Juvenile fiction. | Plankton—Juvenile fiction. | Schools—Juvenile fiction. | Friendship—Juvenile fiction. | Humorous stories. | CYAC: Crabs—Fiction. | Plankton Fiction. | Schools—Fiction. | Friendship—Fiction. | Humorous stories. | LCGFT: Humorous fiction.
Classification: LCC PZ7.F34843 Sc 2022 (print) | DDC [E]—dc23
LC record available at https://lccn.loc.gov/2021051269

10 9 8 7 6 5 4 3 2 1   22 23 24 25 26

Printed in China   62

First edition, June 2022
Edited by Katie Heit
Book design by Sarah Dvojack

THE SCHOOL

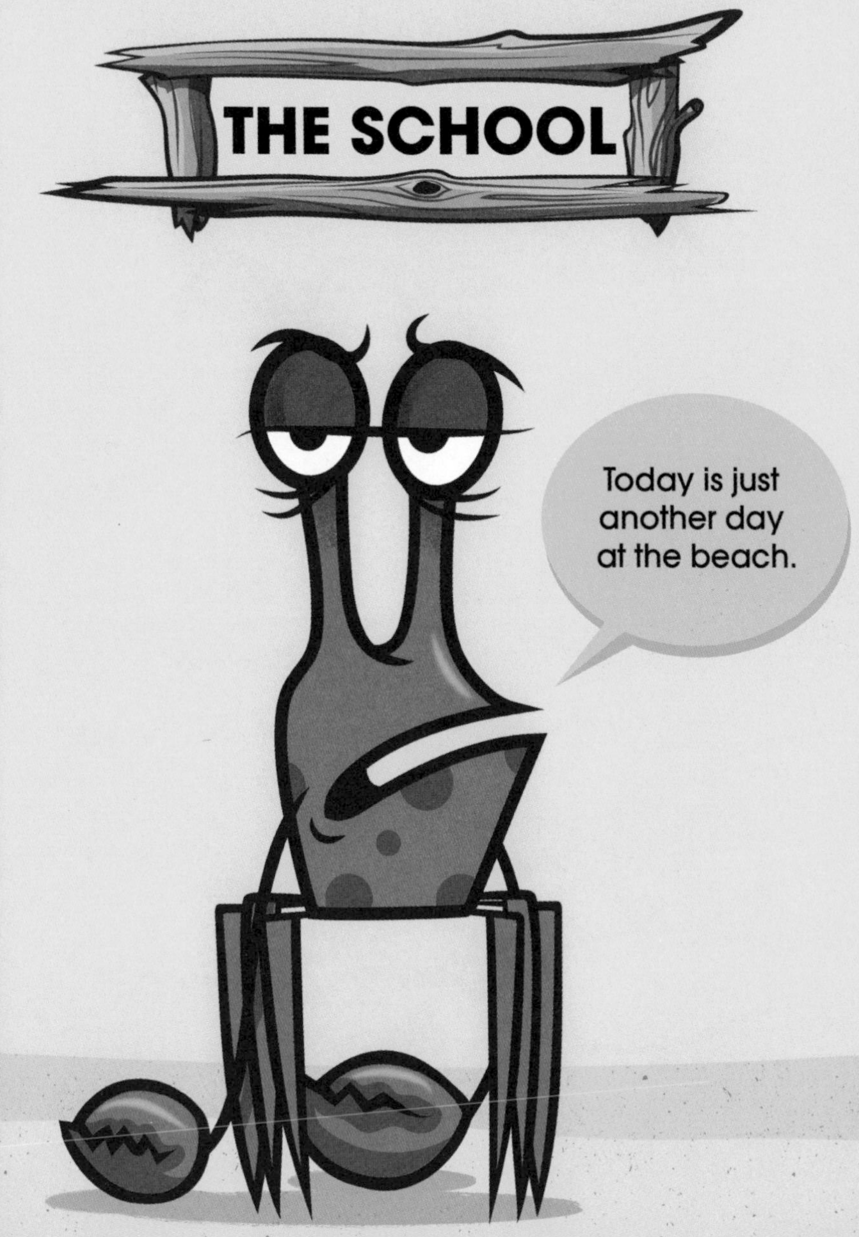
Today is just another day at the beach.

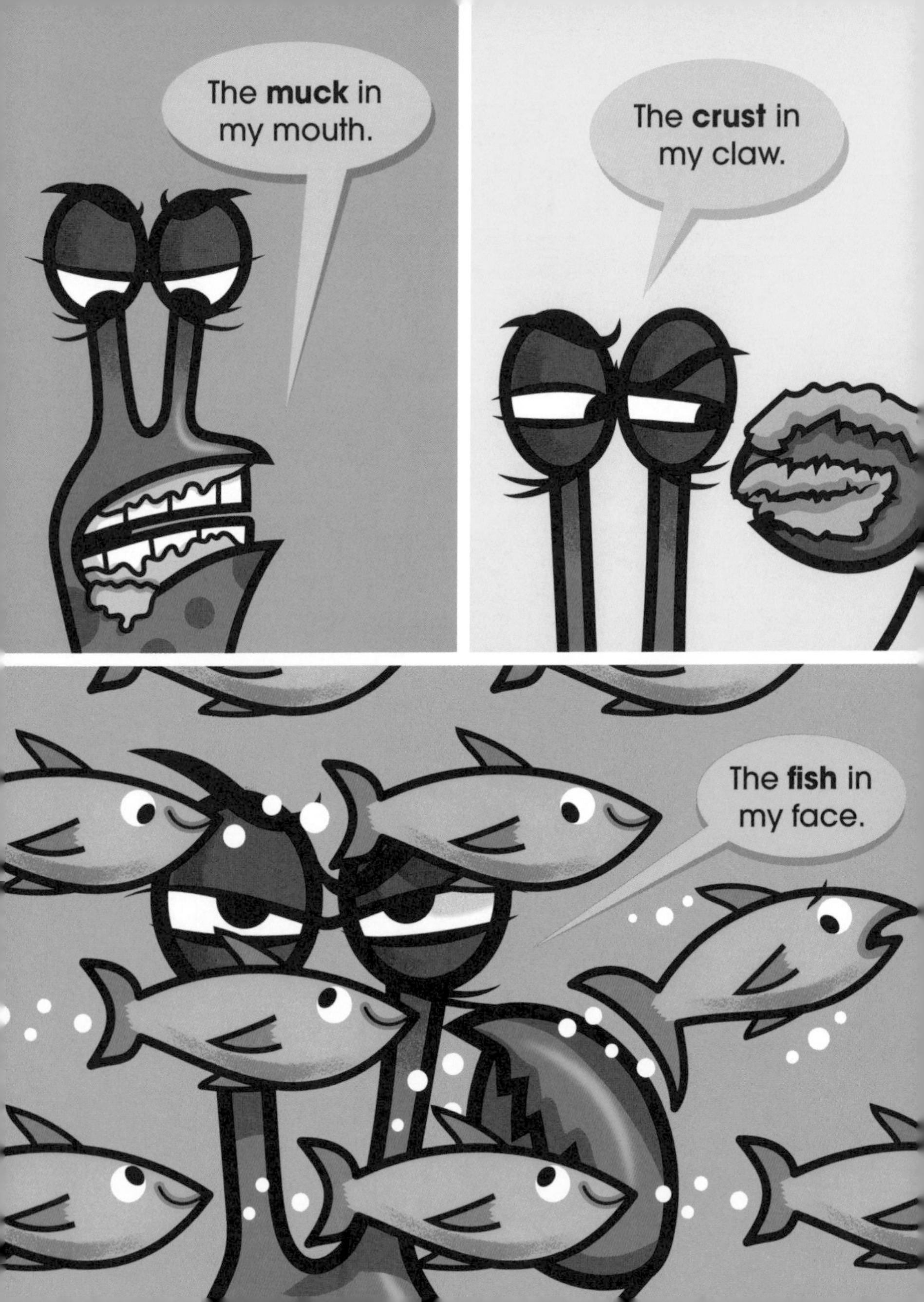
The **muck** in my mouth.
The **crust** in my claw.
The **fish** in my face.

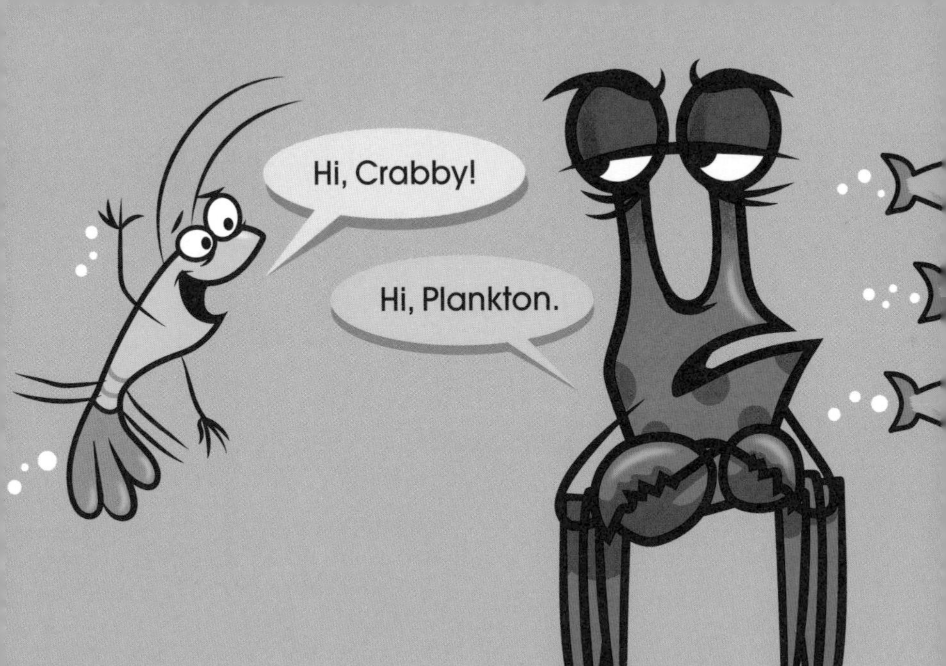
Hi, Crabby!
Hi, Plankton.

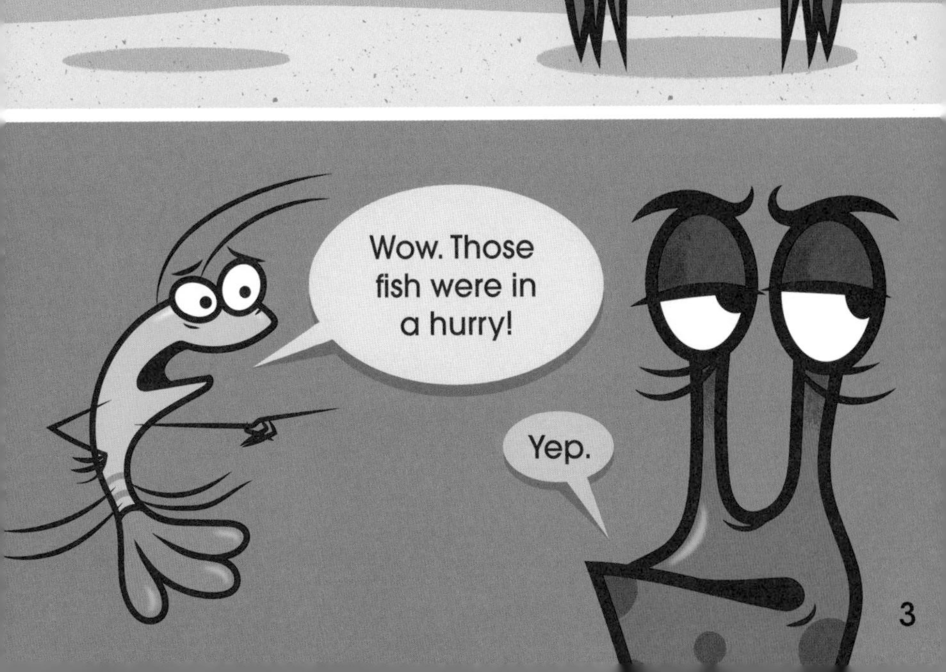
Wow. Those fish were in a hurry!
Yep.

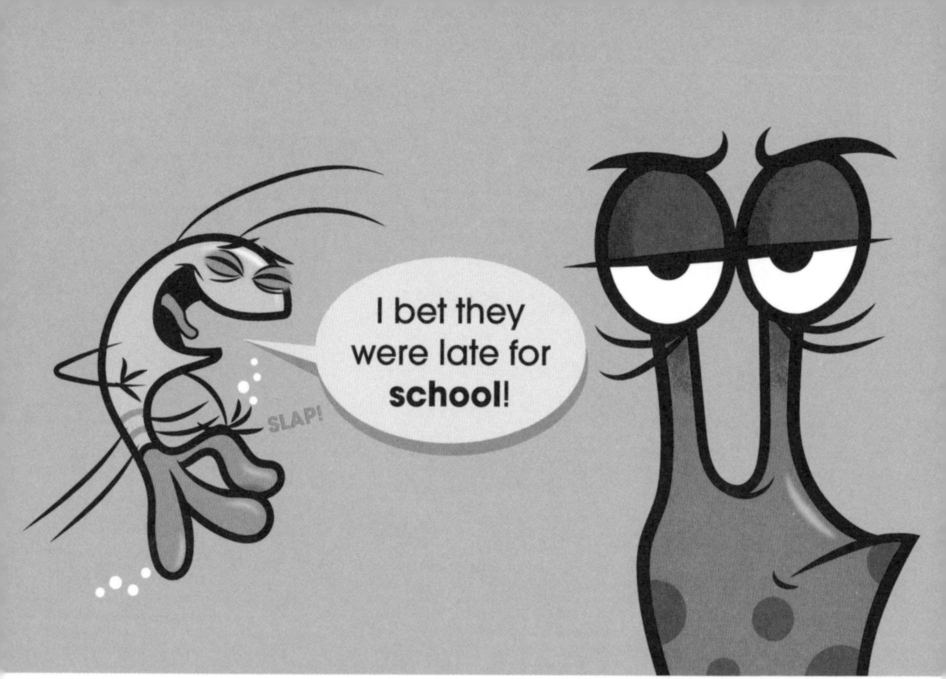
I bet they were late for **school**!
SLAP!

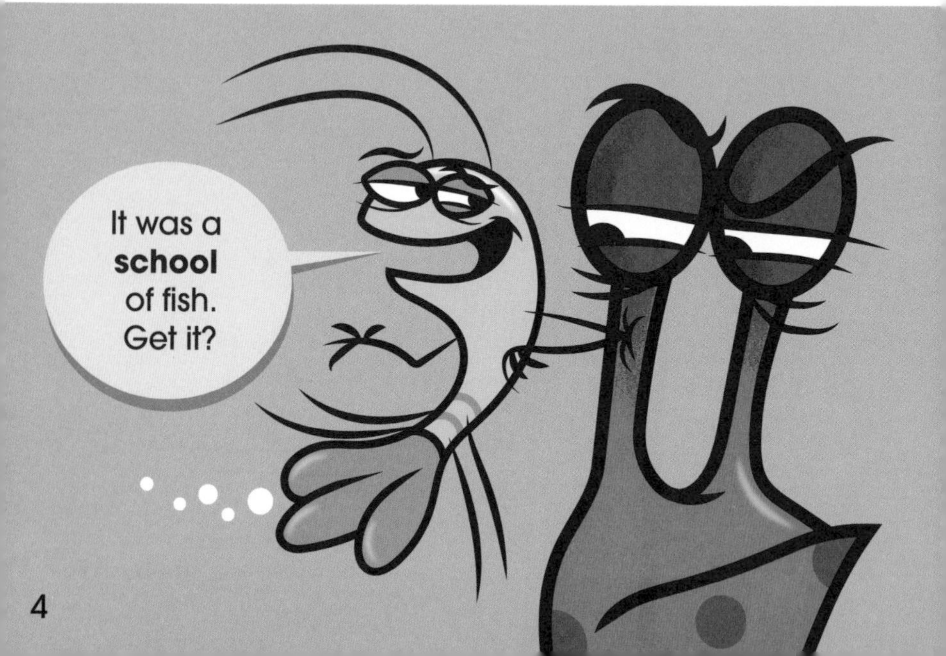
It was a **school** of fish. Get it?

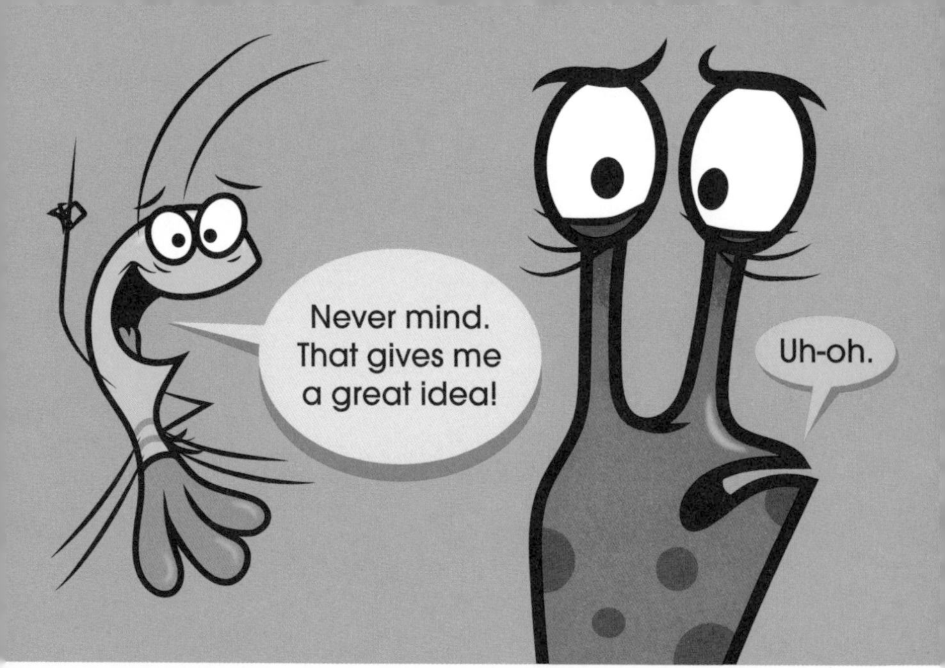
Never mind. That gives me a great idea!
Uh-oh.

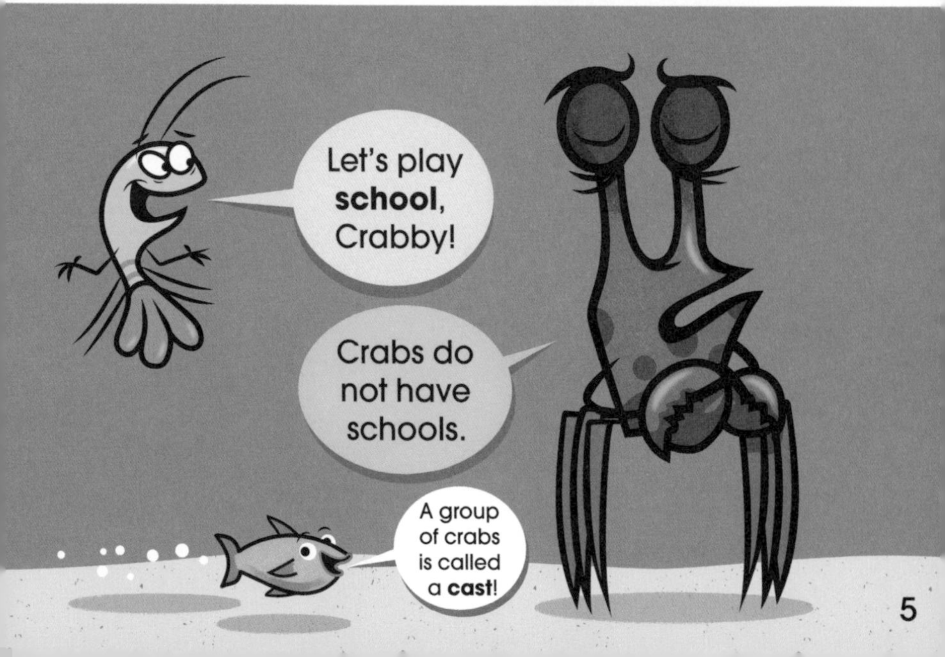
Let's play **school**, Crabby!
Crabs do not have schools.
A group of crabs is called a **cast**!

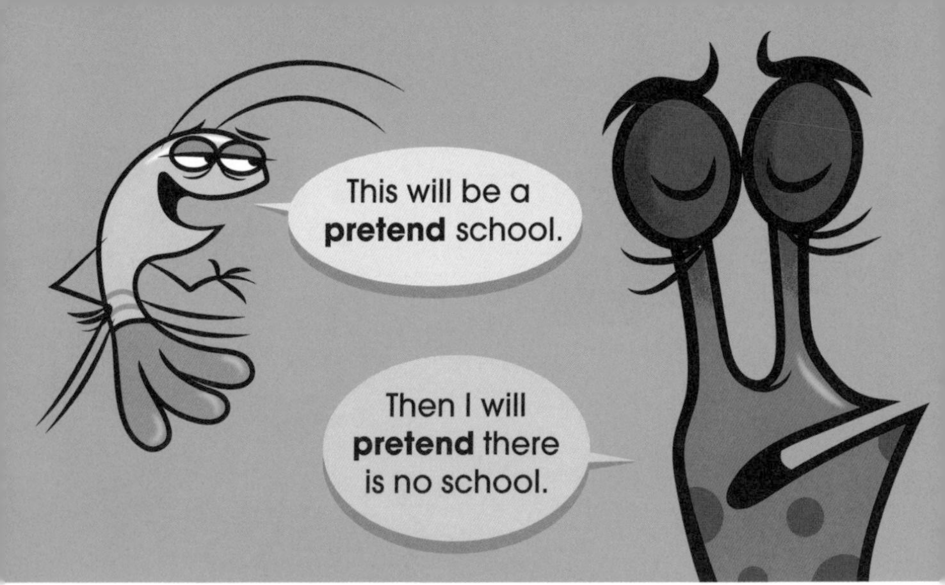
This will be a **pretend** school.
Then I will **pretend** there is no school.

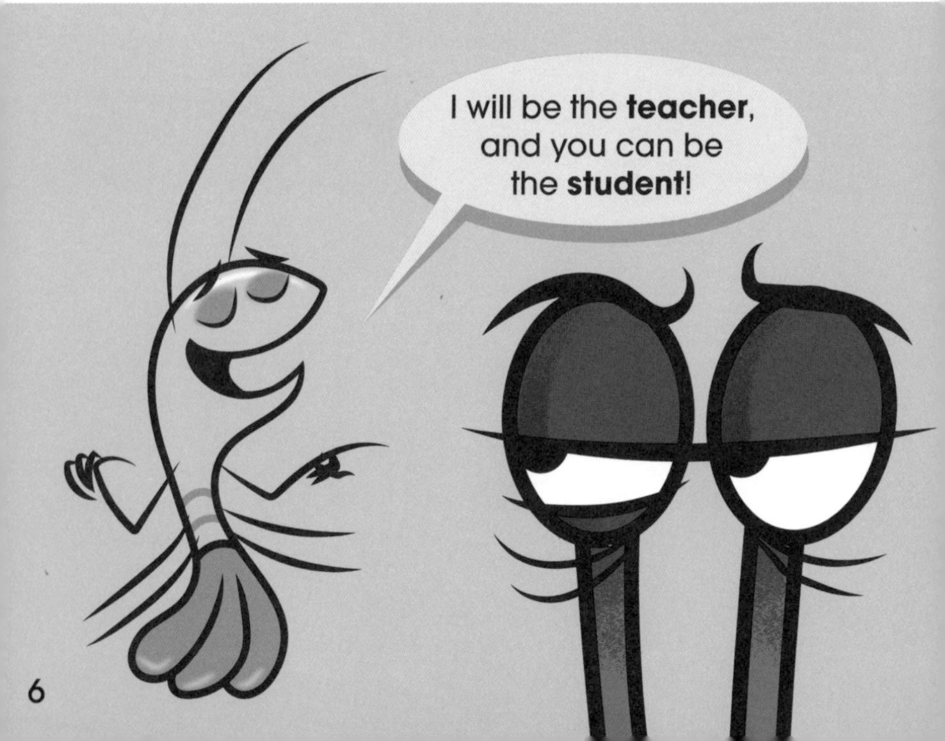
I will be the **teacher**, and you can be the **student**!

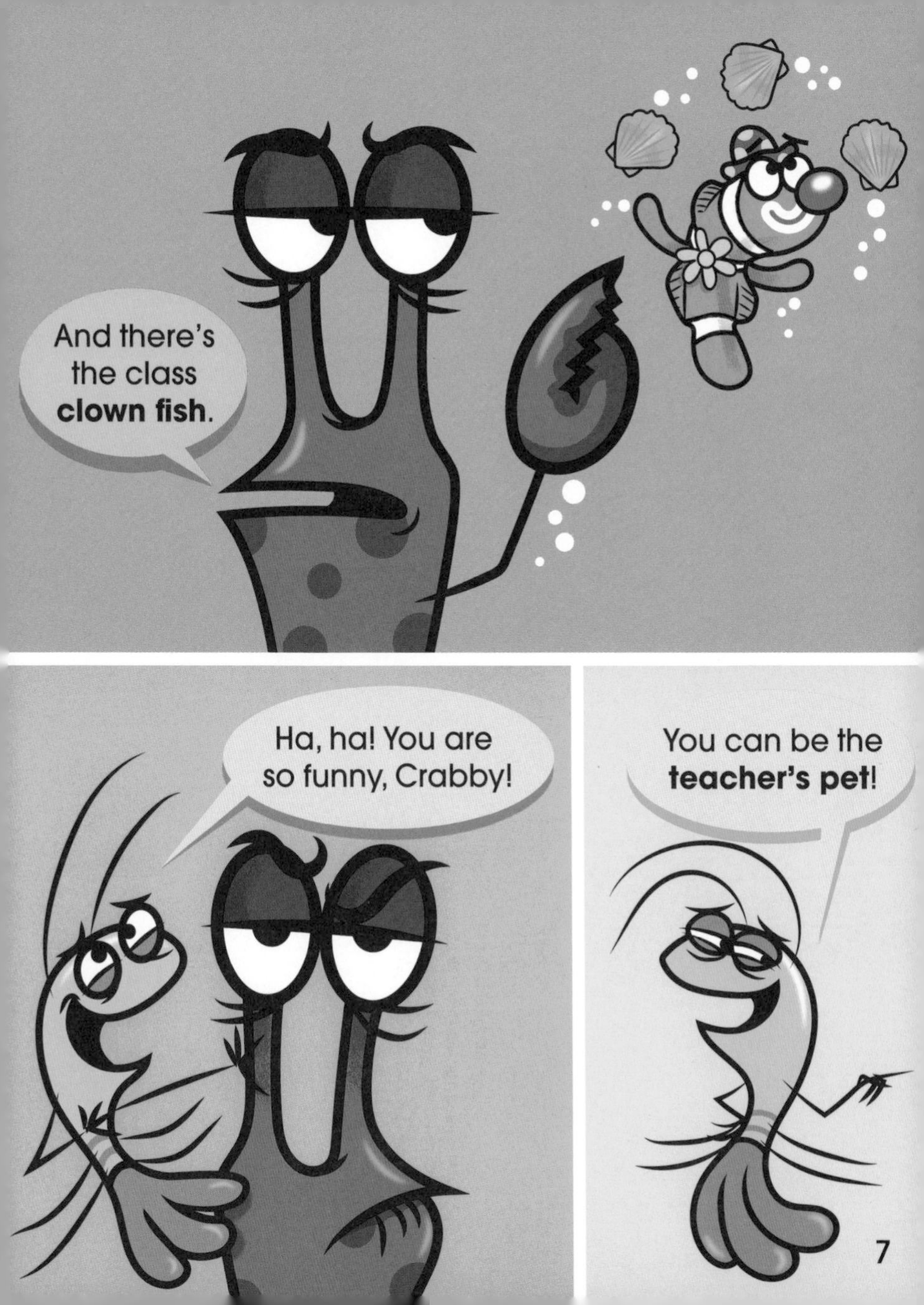

And there's the class **clown fish**.
Ha, ha! You are so funny, Crabby!
You can be the **teacher's pet**!

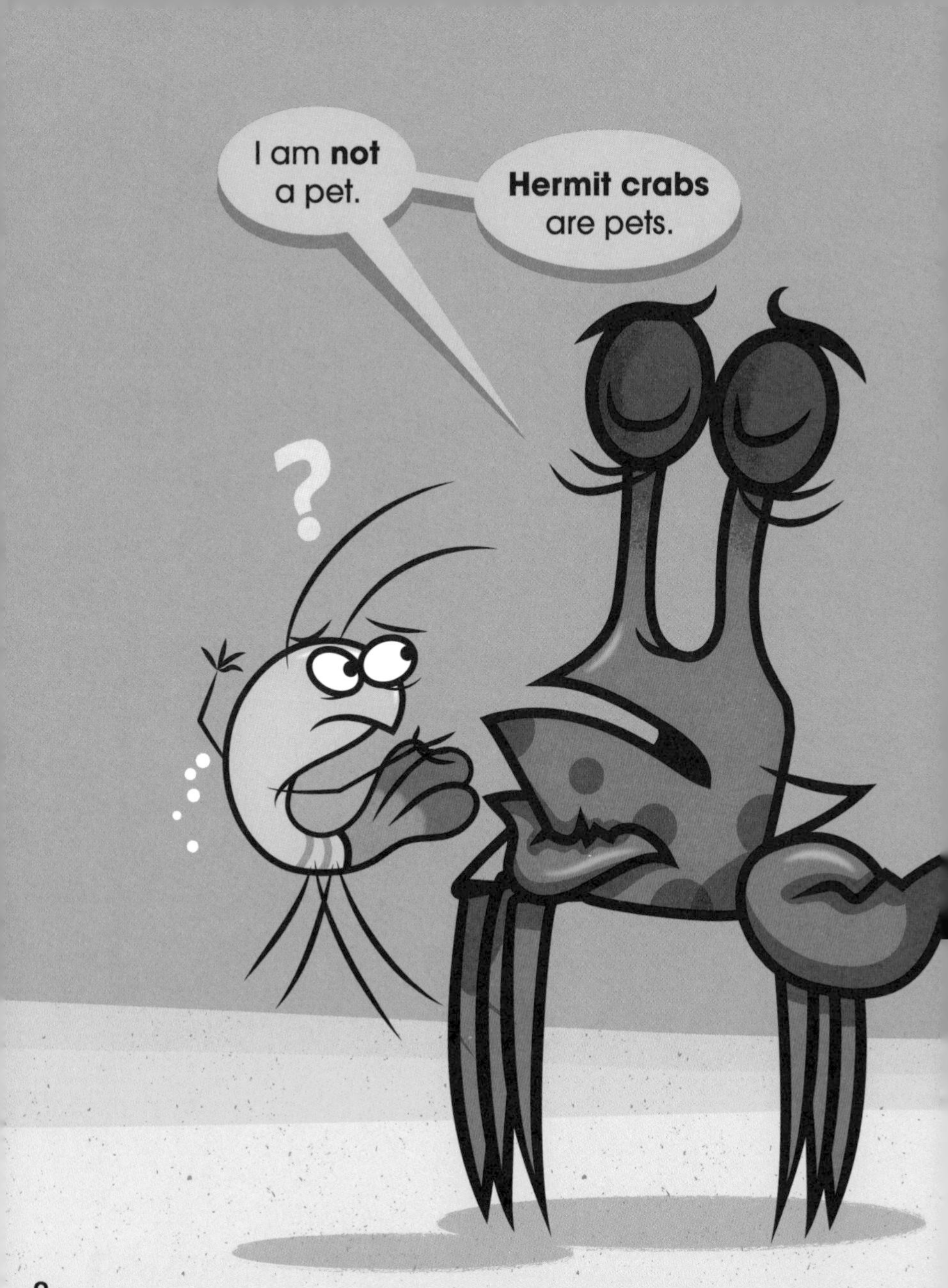
I am **not** a pet.
Hermit crabs are pets.

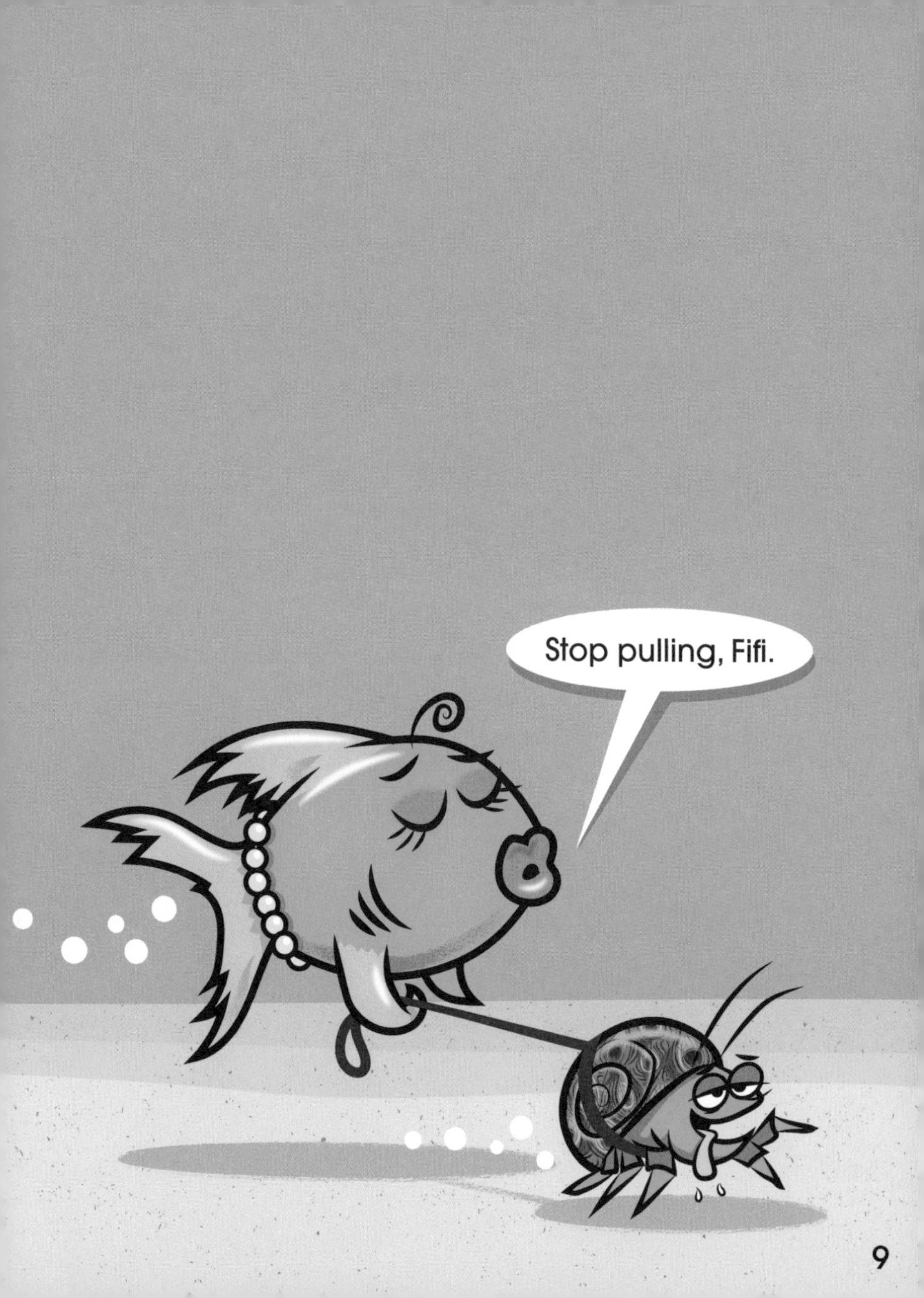
Stop pulling, Fifi.

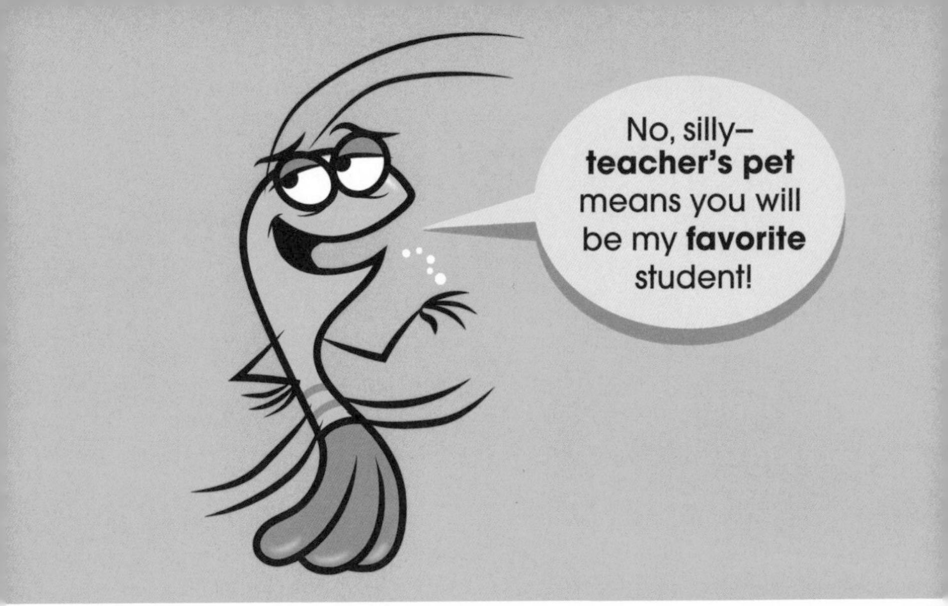
No, silly–
teacher's pet means you will be my **favorite** student!

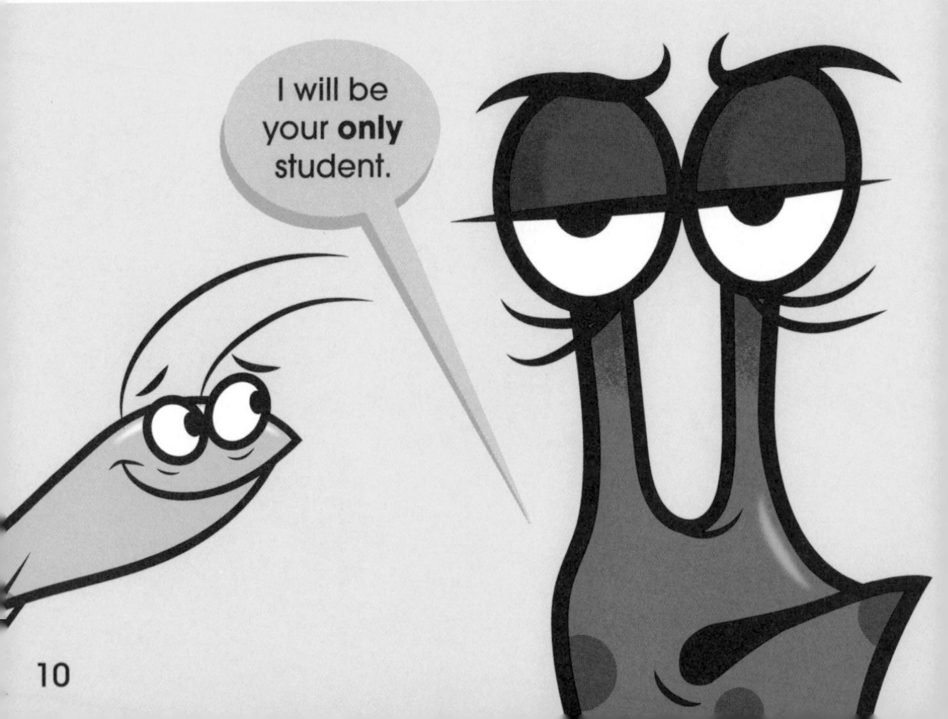
I will be your **only** student.

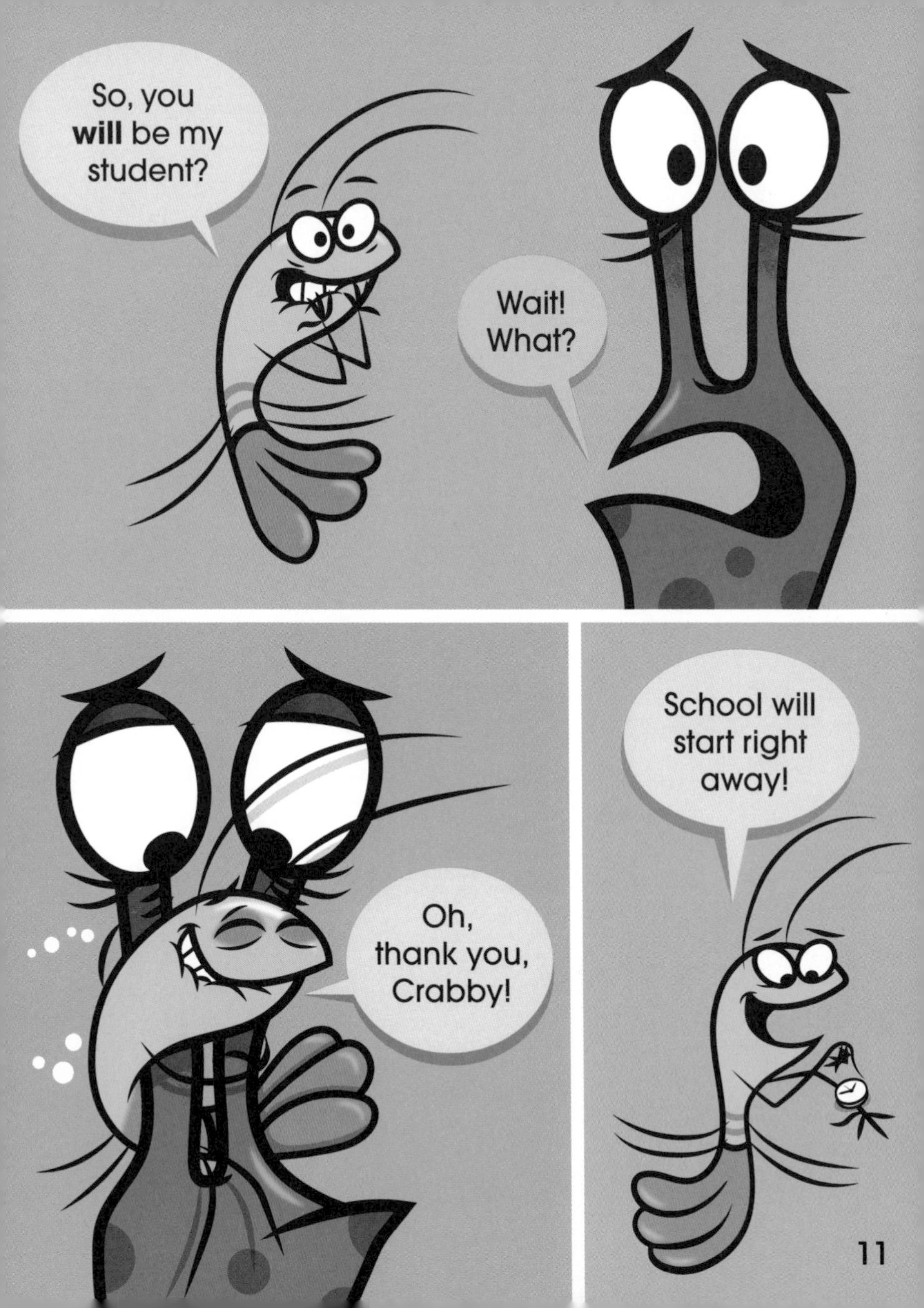
So, you **will** be my student?
Wait! What?
Oh, thank you, Crabby!
School will start right away!

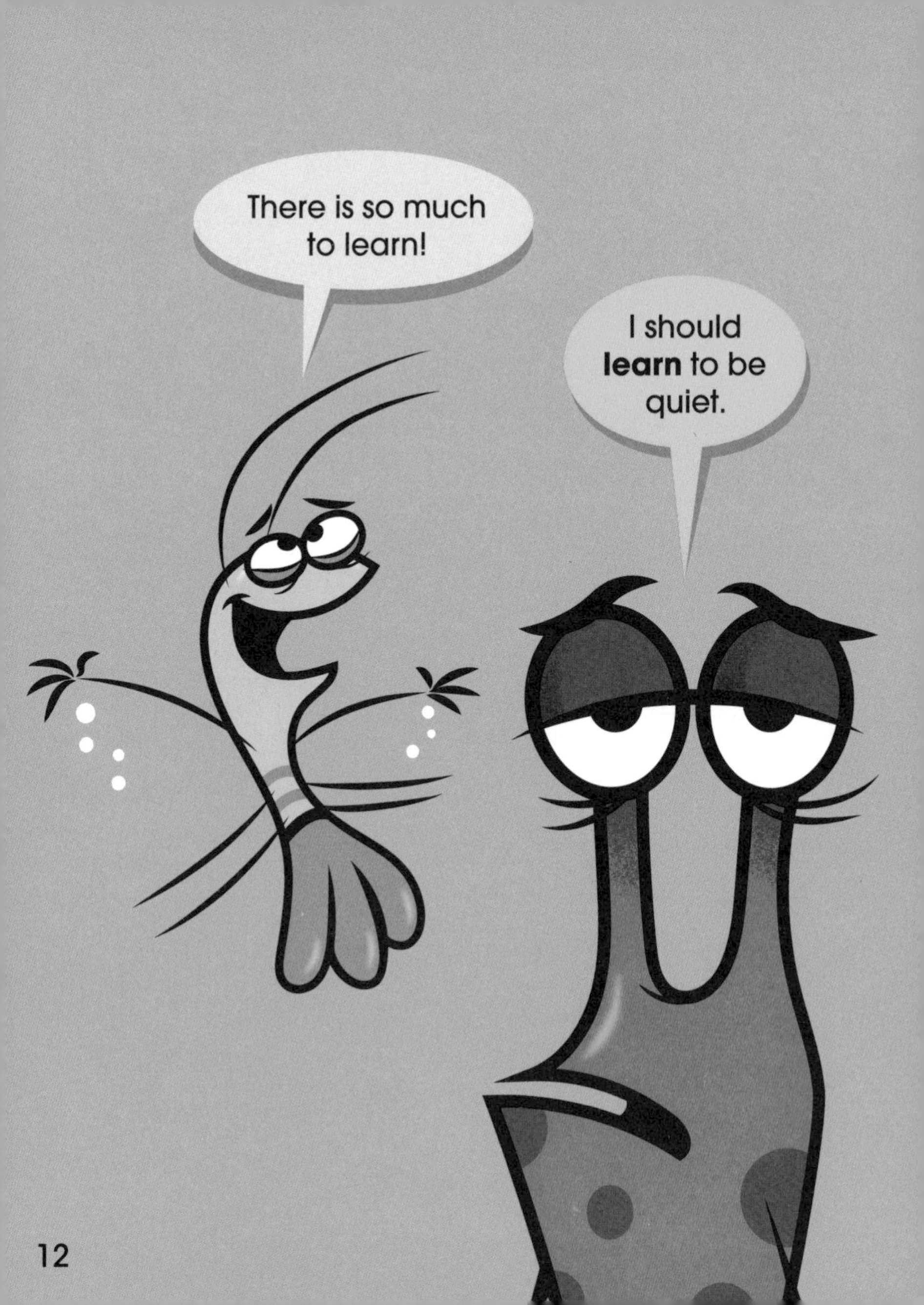
There is so much to learn!
I should **learn** to be quiet.

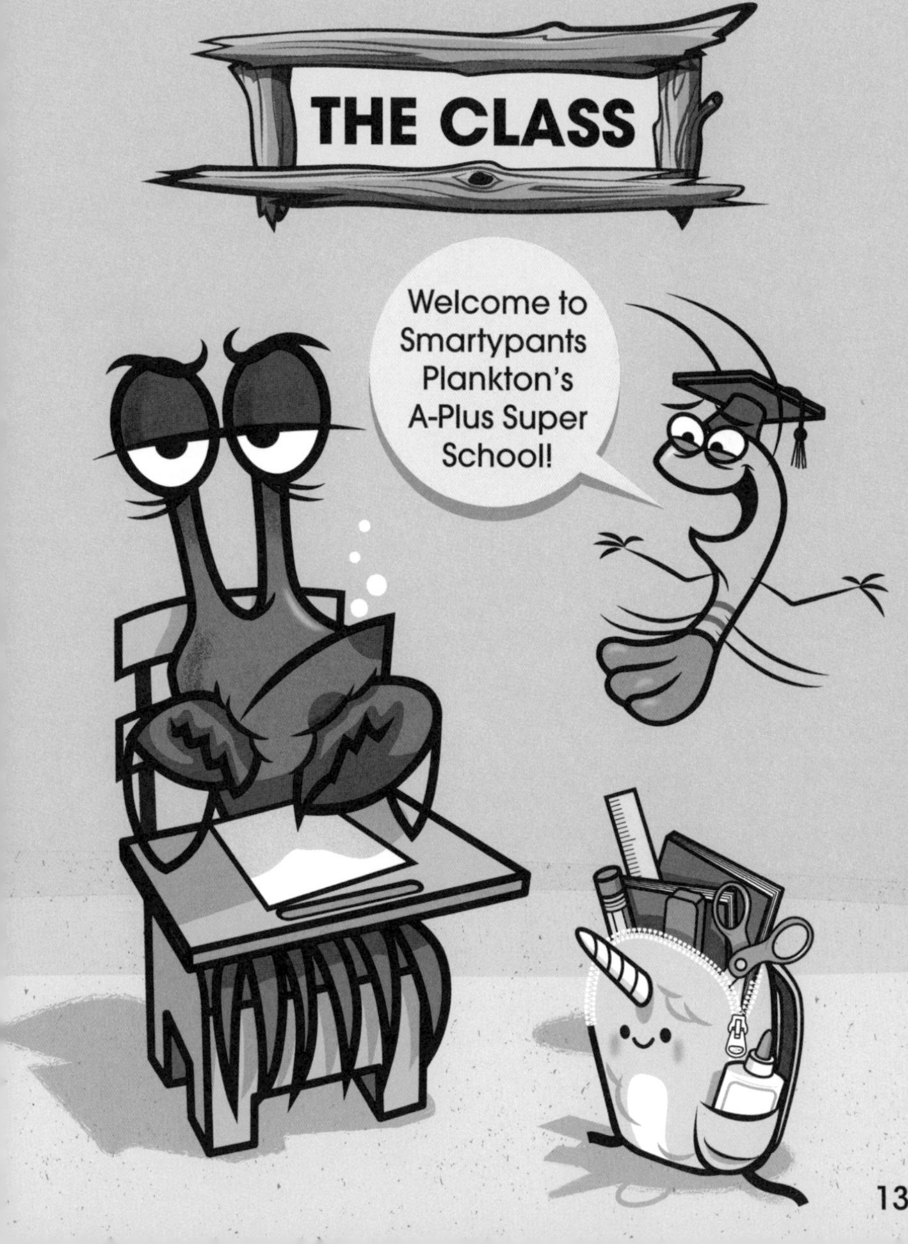
THE CLASS
Welcome to Smartypants Plankton's A-Plus Super School!

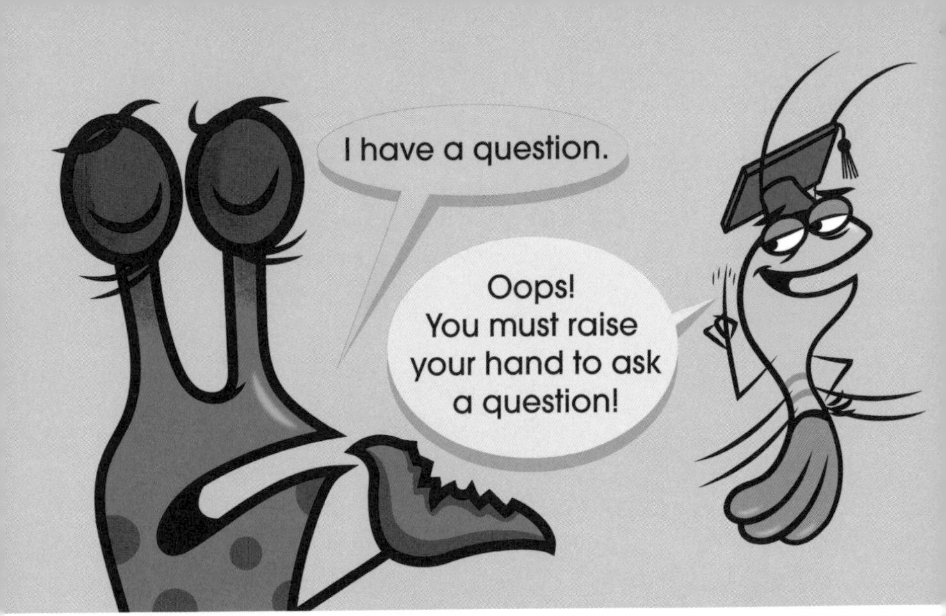
I have a question.
Oops! You must raise your hand to ask a question!

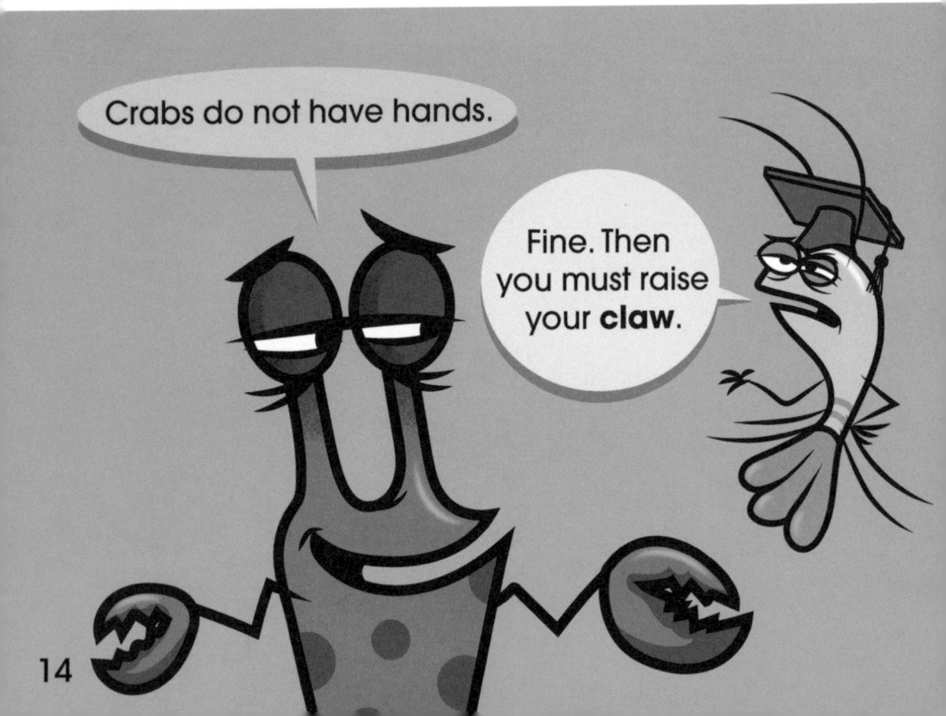
Crabs do not have hands.
Fine. Then you must raise your **claw**.

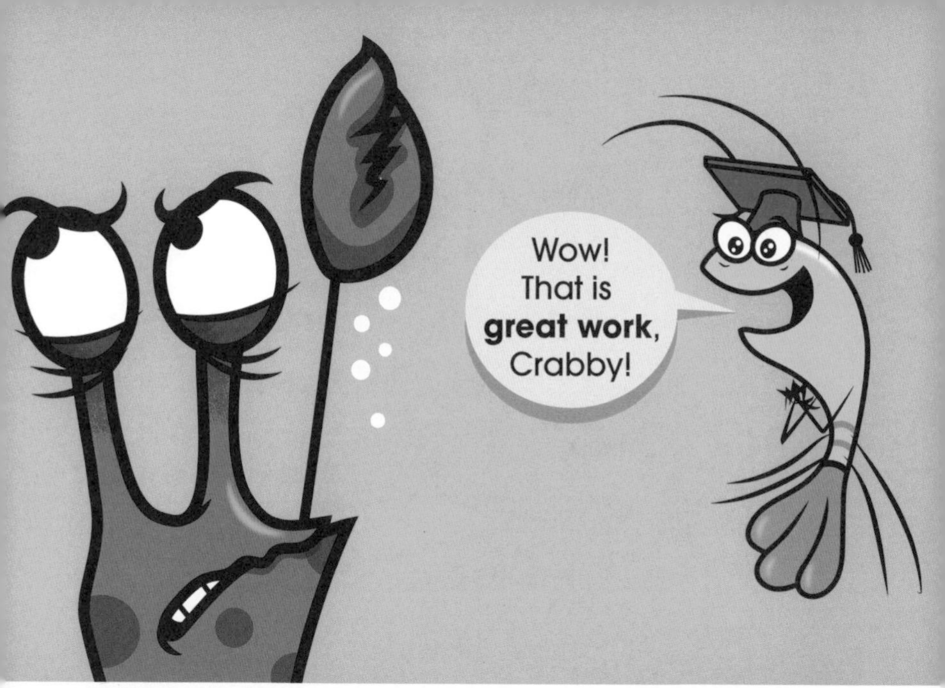
Wow! That is **great work**, Crabby!

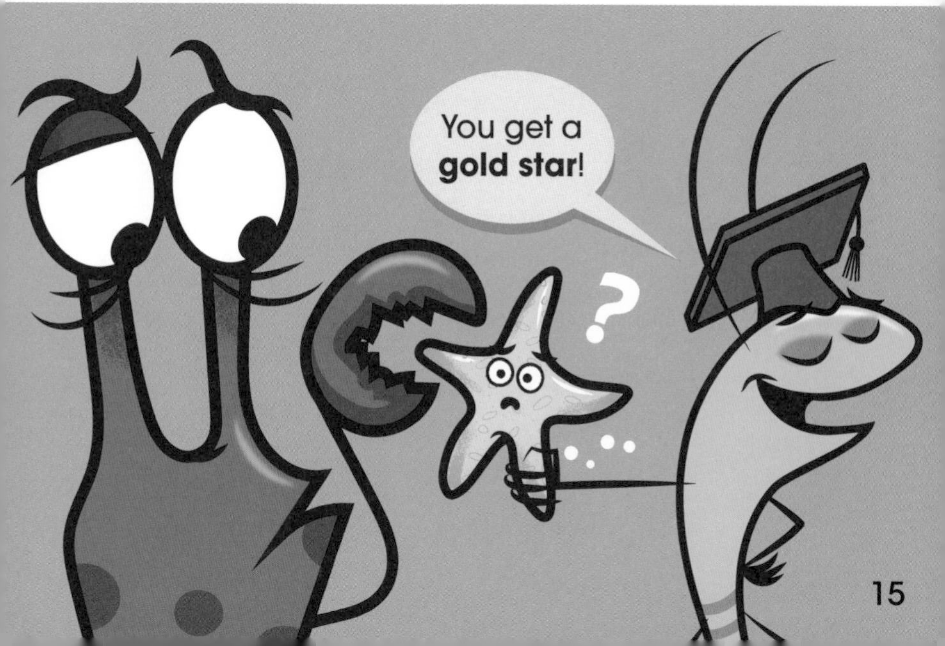
You get a **gold star**!
?

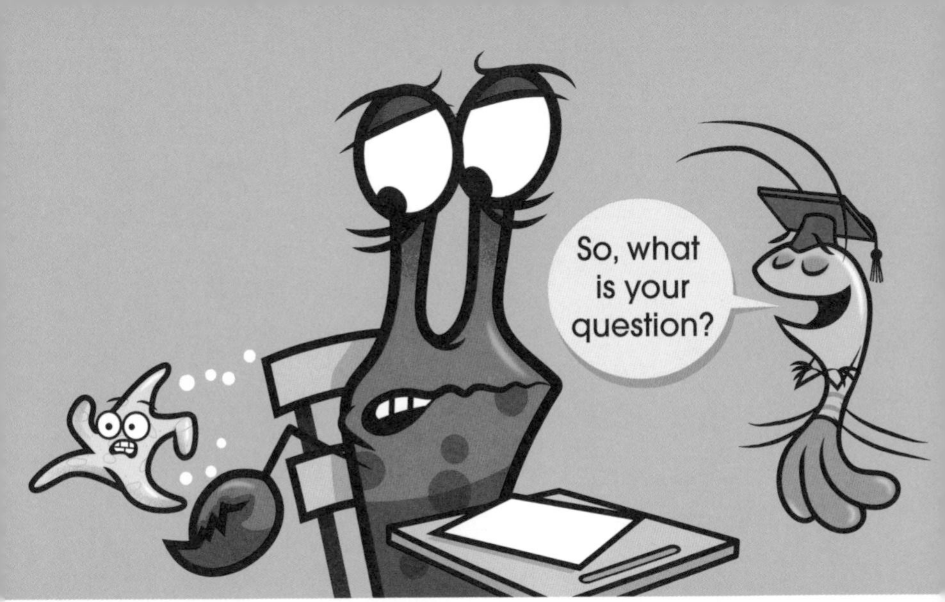
So, what is your question?

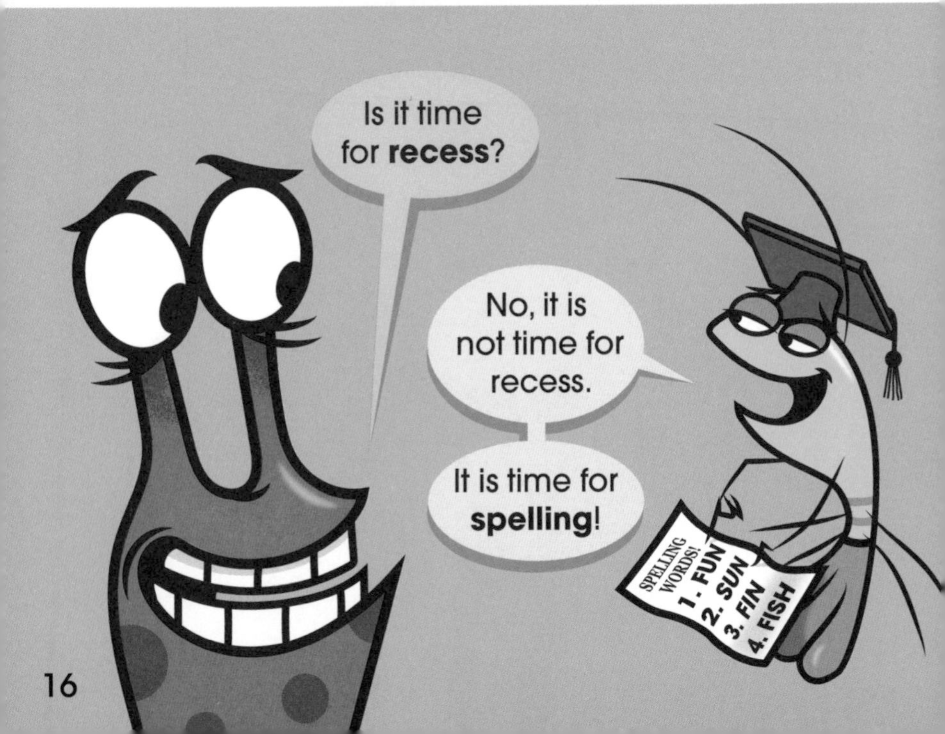
Is it time for **recess**?
No, it is not time for recess.
It is time for **spelling**!
SPELLING WORDS!
1. FUN
2. SUN
3. FIN
4. FISH

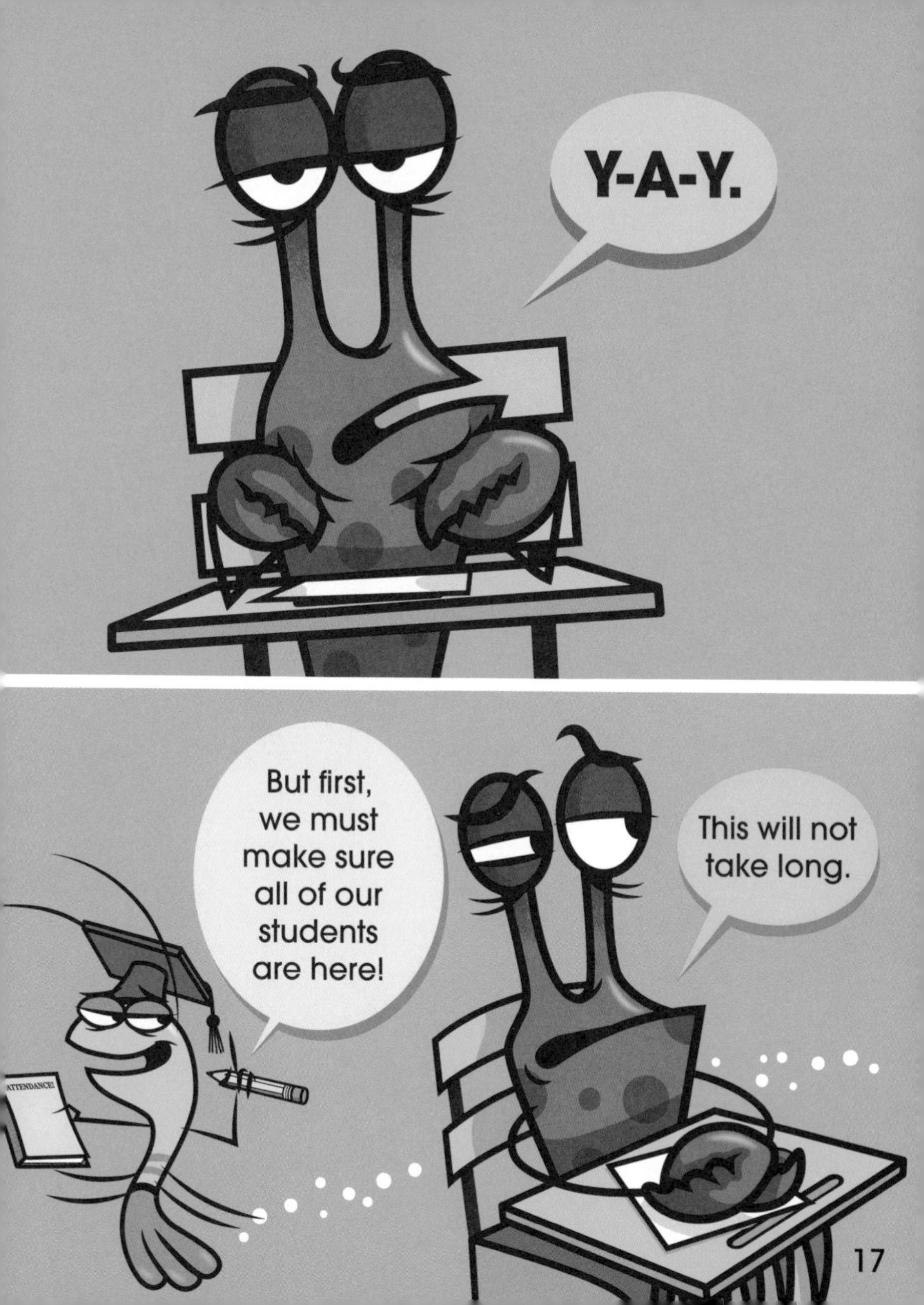
Y-A-Y.
But first, we must make sure all of our students are here!
ATTENDANCE!
This will not take long.

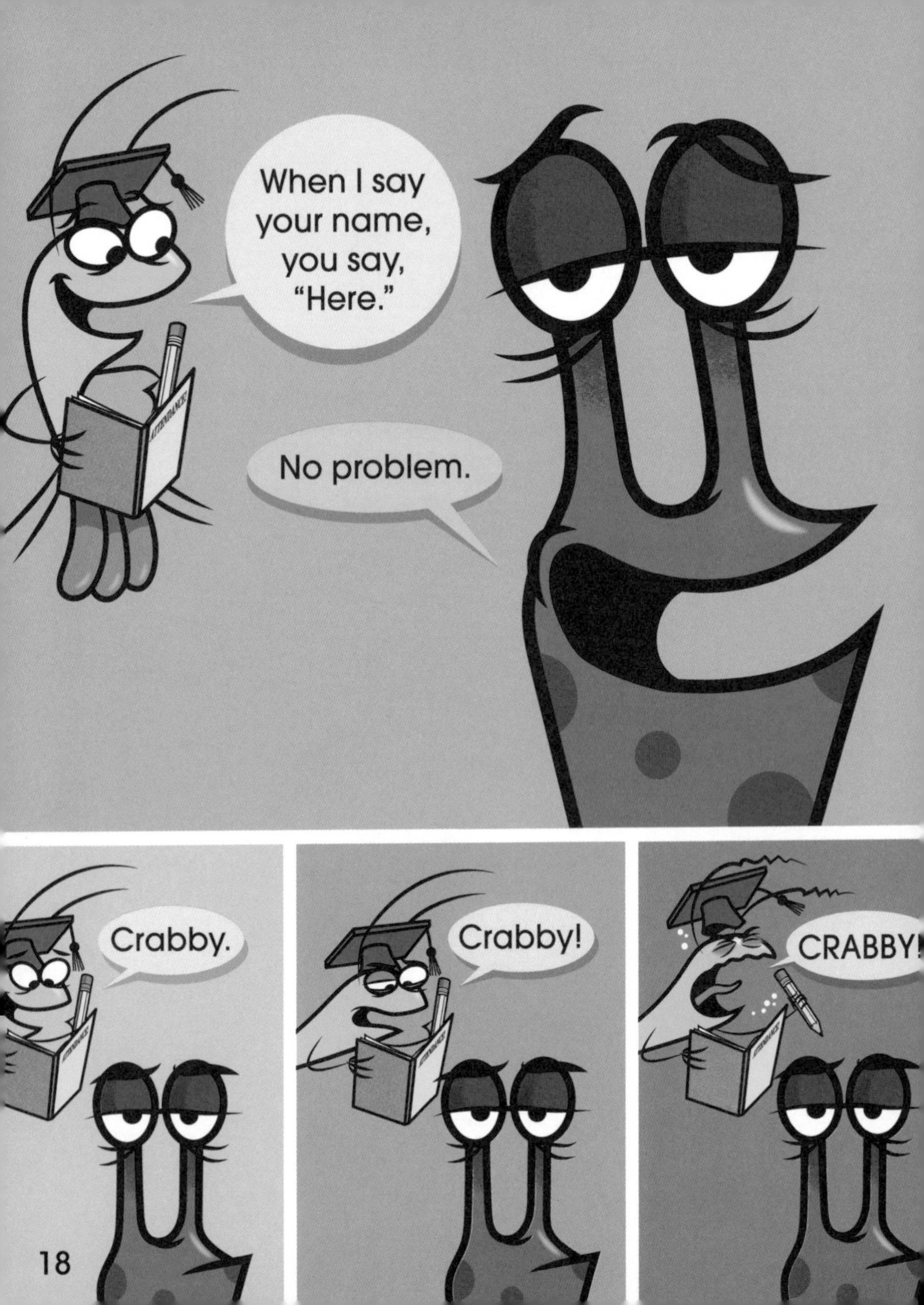
When I say your name, you say, "Here."
No problem.
Crabby.
Crabby!
CRABBY!

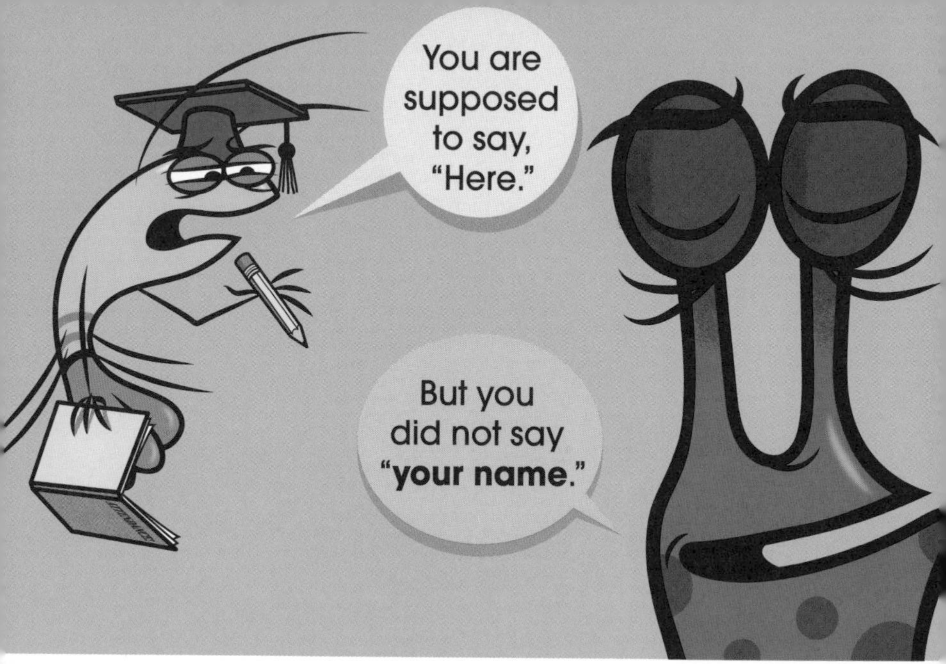
You are supposed to say, "Here."
But you did not say **"your name."**

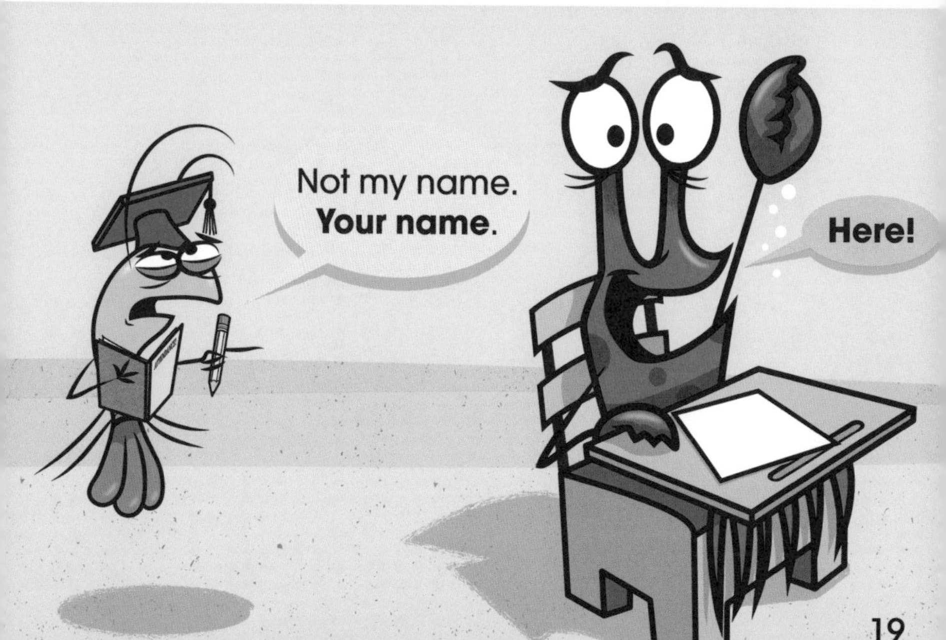
Not my name. **Your name.**
Here!

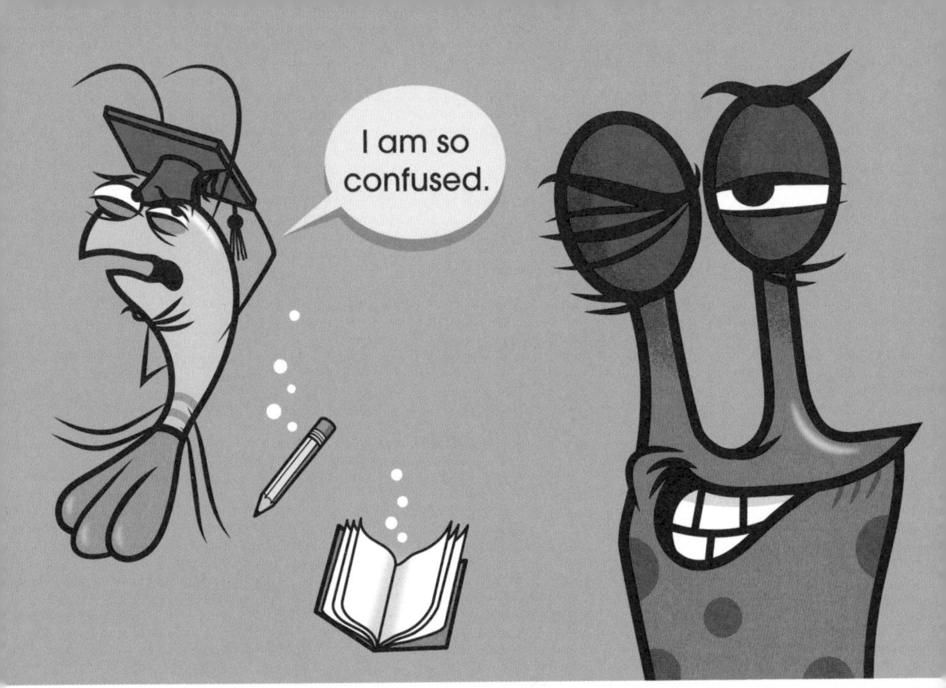
I am so confused.

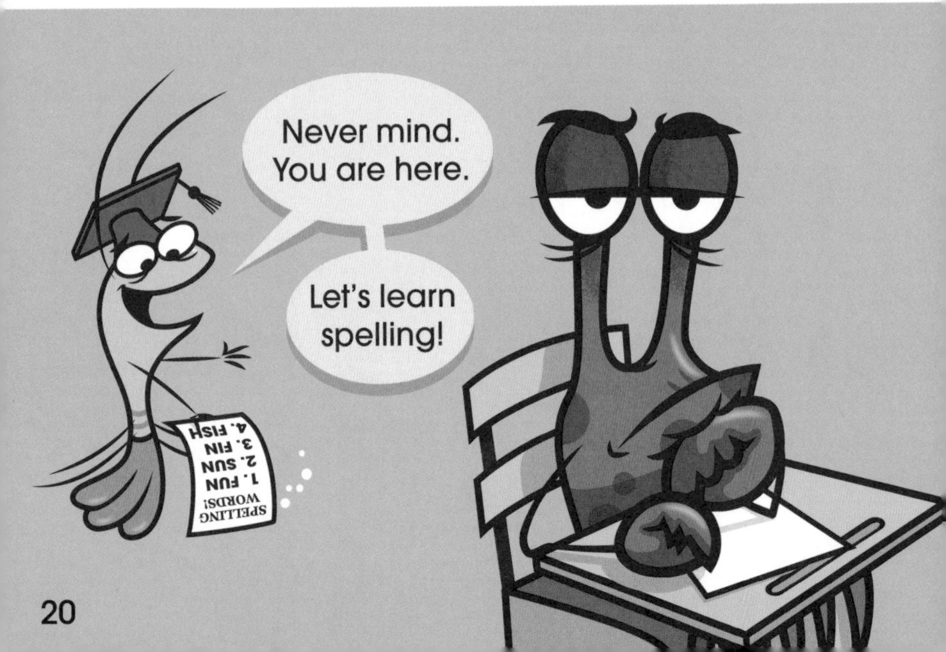
Never mind. You are here.
Let's learn spelling!
SPELLING WORDS!
1. FUN
2. SUN
3. FIN
4. FISH

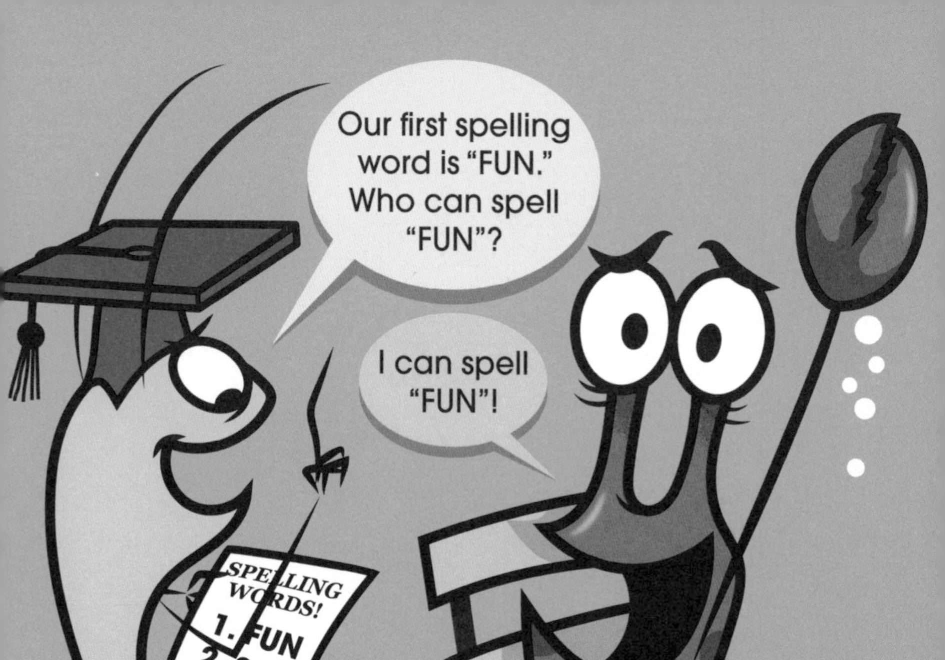
Our first spelling word is "FUN." Who can spell "FUN"?
I can spell "FUN"!
SPELLING WORDS!
1. FUN
2. SUN
3. FIN
4. FISH

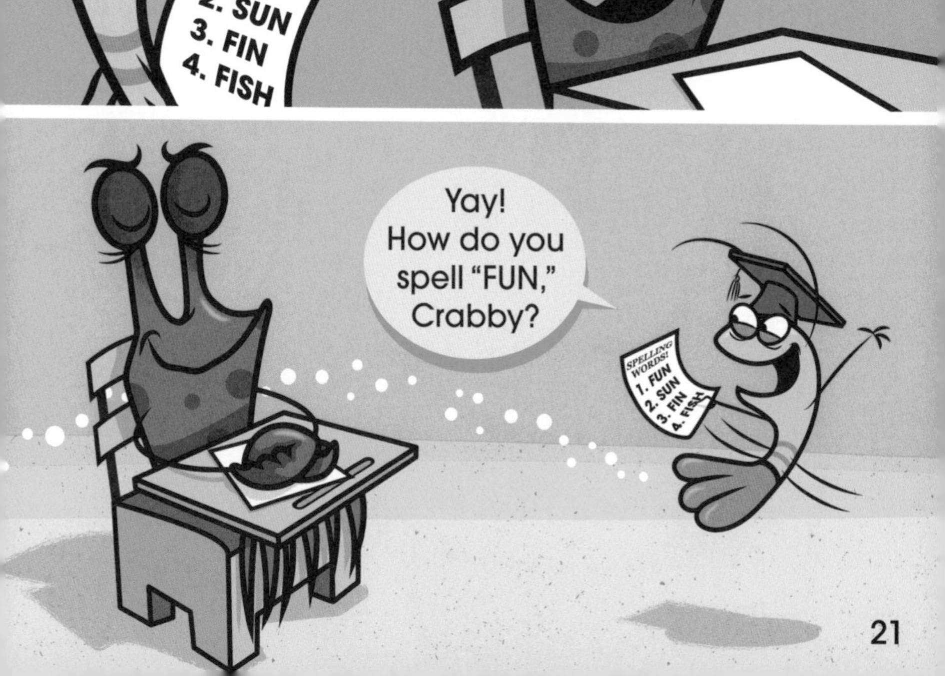
Yay! How do you spell "FUN," Crabby?
SPELLING WORDS!
1. FUN
2. SUN
3. FIN
4. FISH

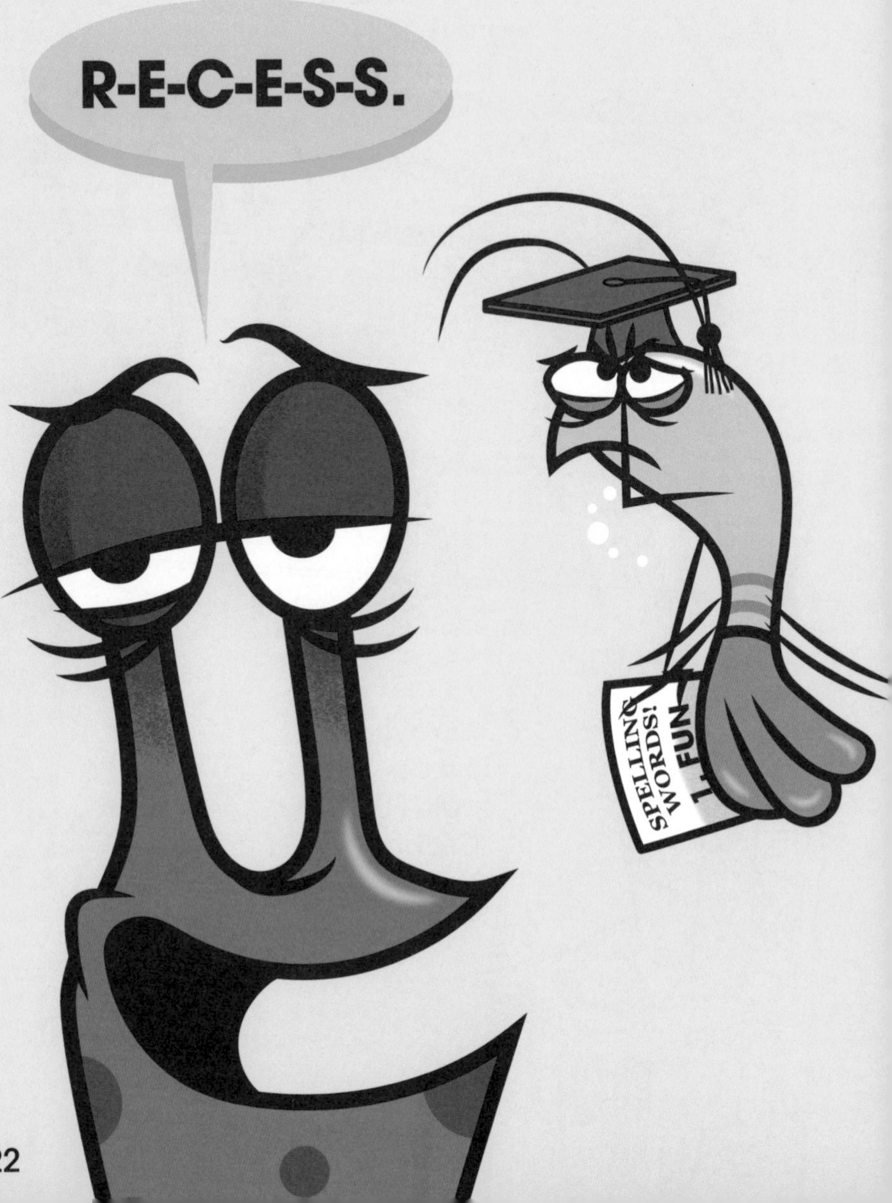
R-E-C-E-S-S.
SPELLING WORDS!
1. FUN

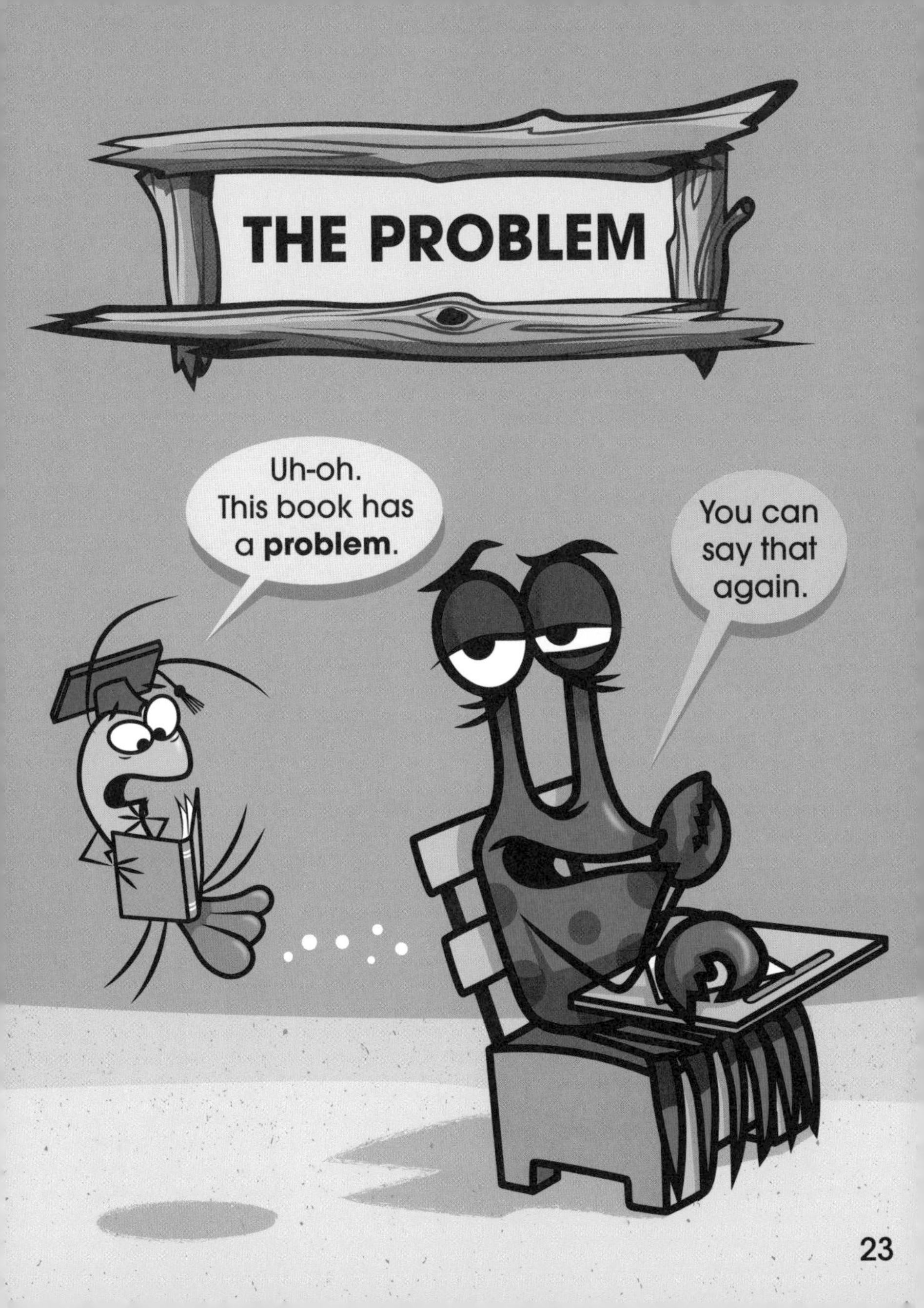
THE PROBLEM
Uh-oh. This book has a **problem**.
You can say that again.
...

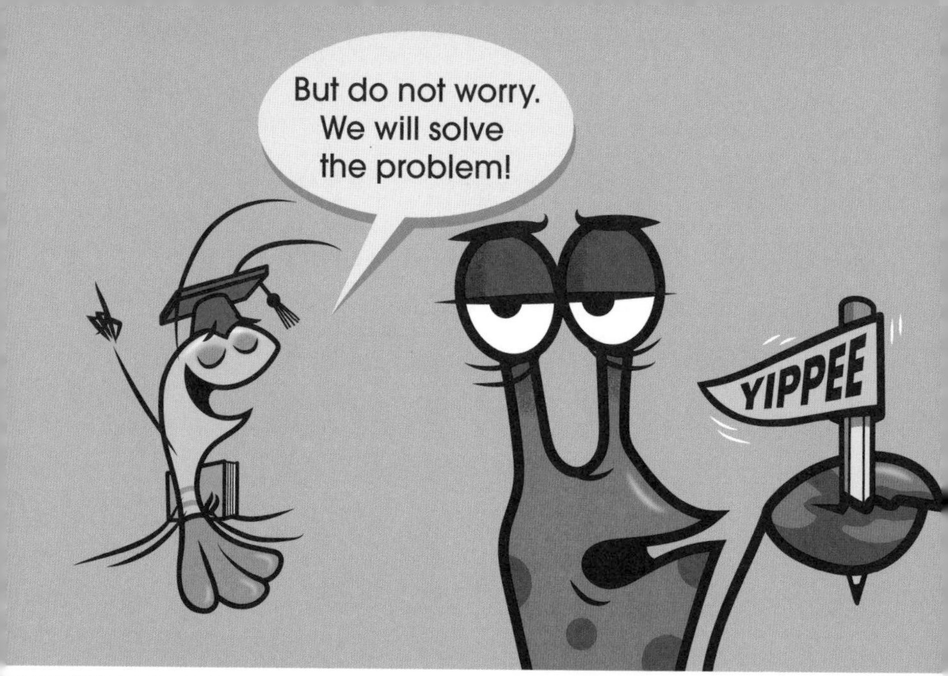
But do not worry. We will solve the problem!
YIPPEE

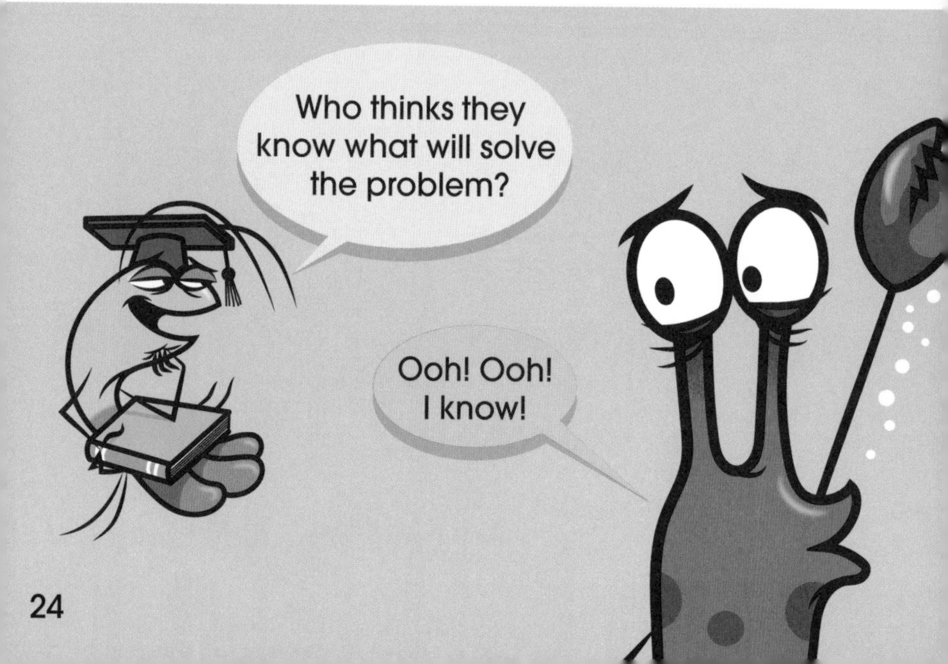
Who thinks they know what will solve the problem?
Ooh! Ooh! I know!

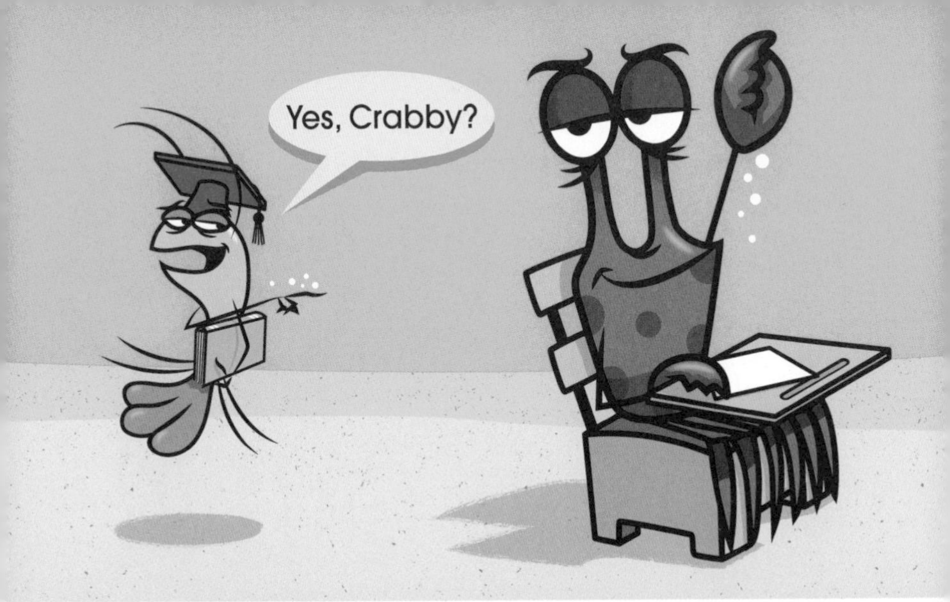
Yes, Crabby?

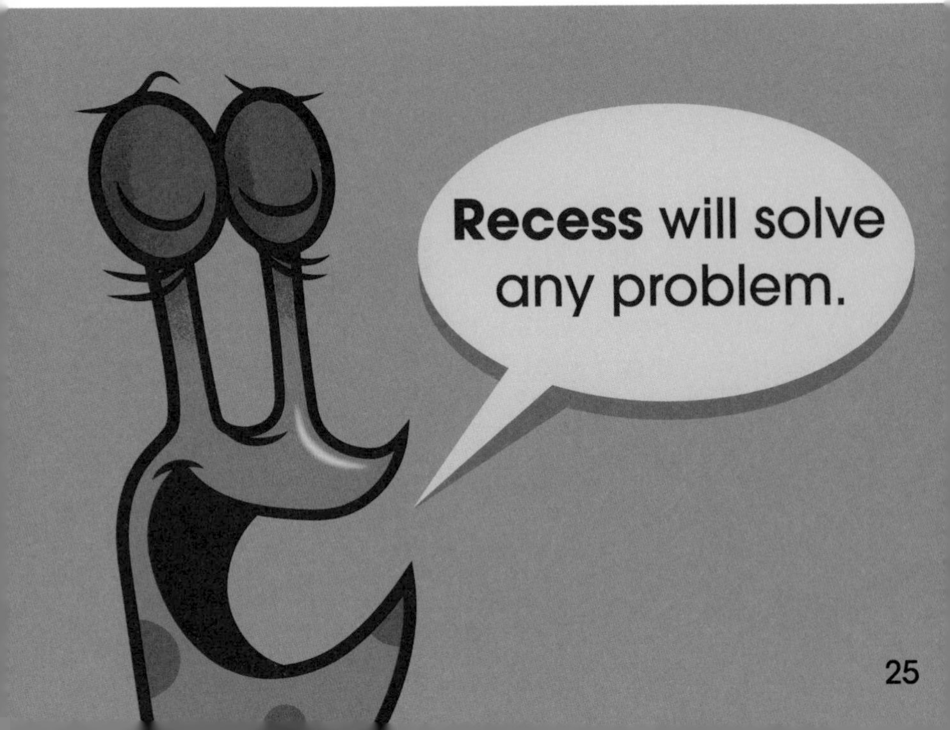
Recess will solve any problem.

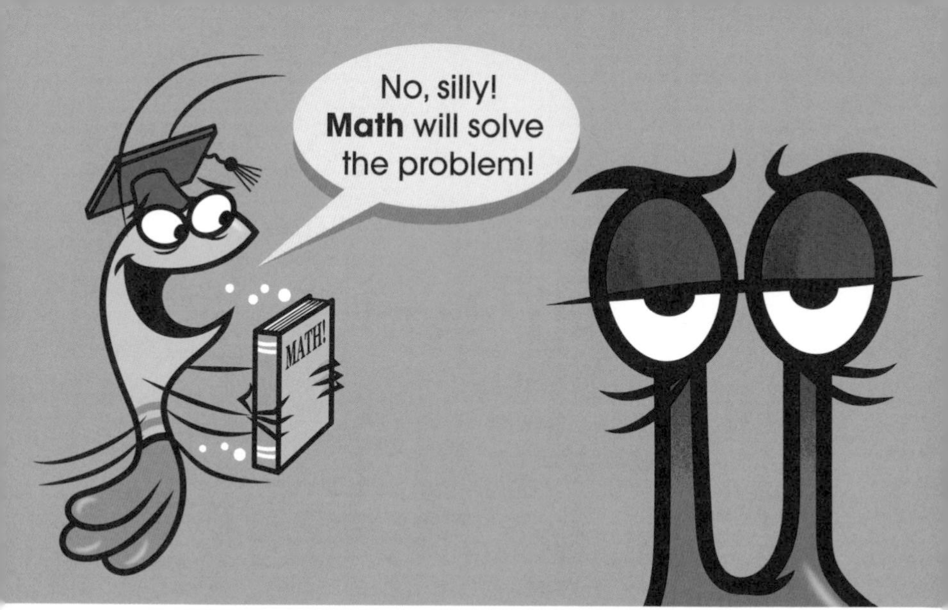
No, silly! **Math** will solve the problem!
MATH!

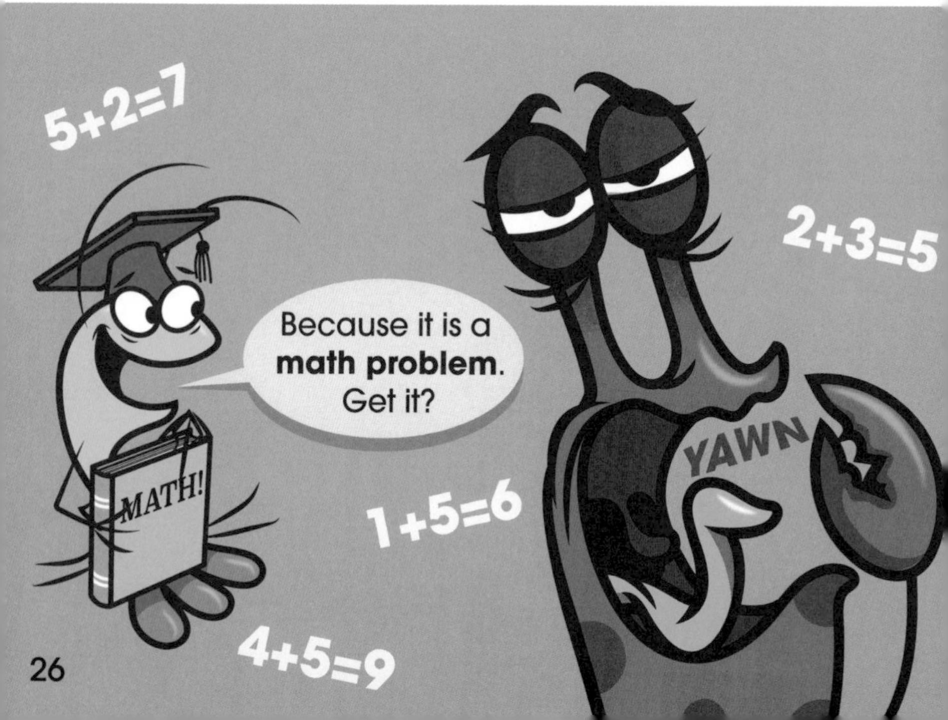
5+2=7
2+3=5
Because it is a **math problem**. Get it?
YAWN
MATH!
1+5=6
4+5=9

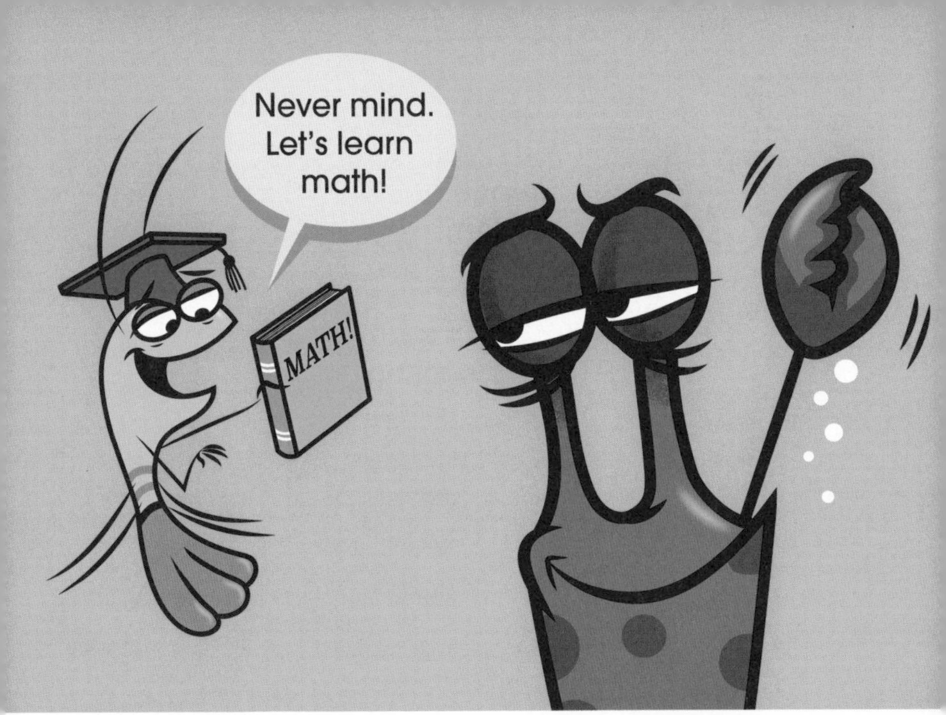
Never mind. Let's learn math!
MATH!

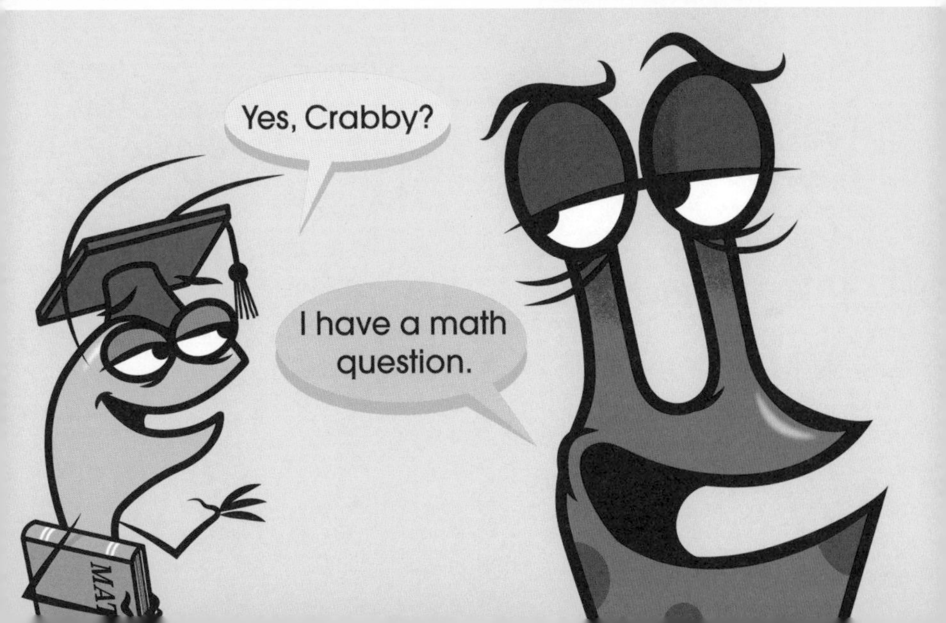
Yes, Crabby?
I have a math question.

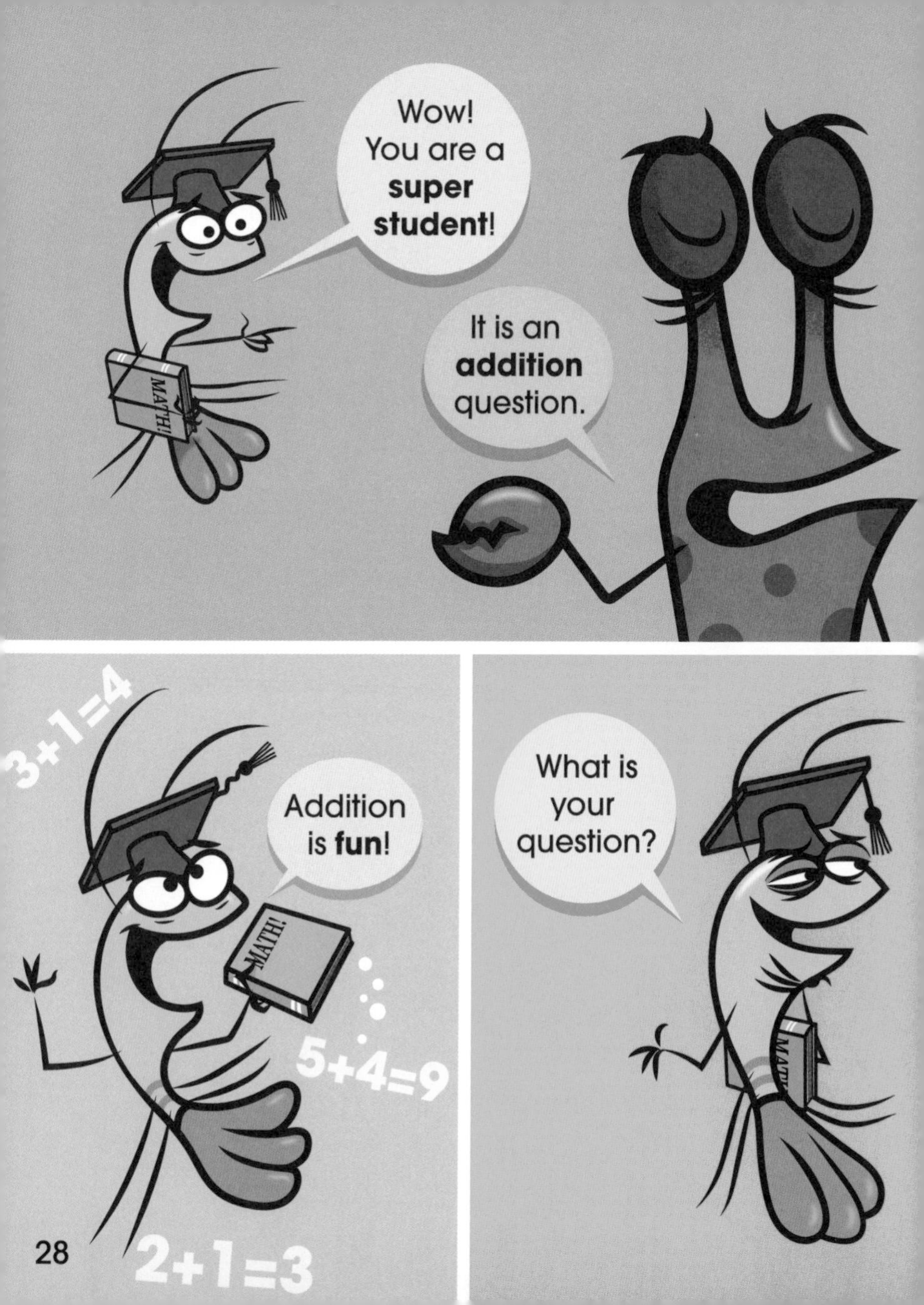
Wow! You are a **super student**!
It is an **addition** question.
3+1=4
Addition is **fun**!
5+4=9
2+1=3
What is your question?

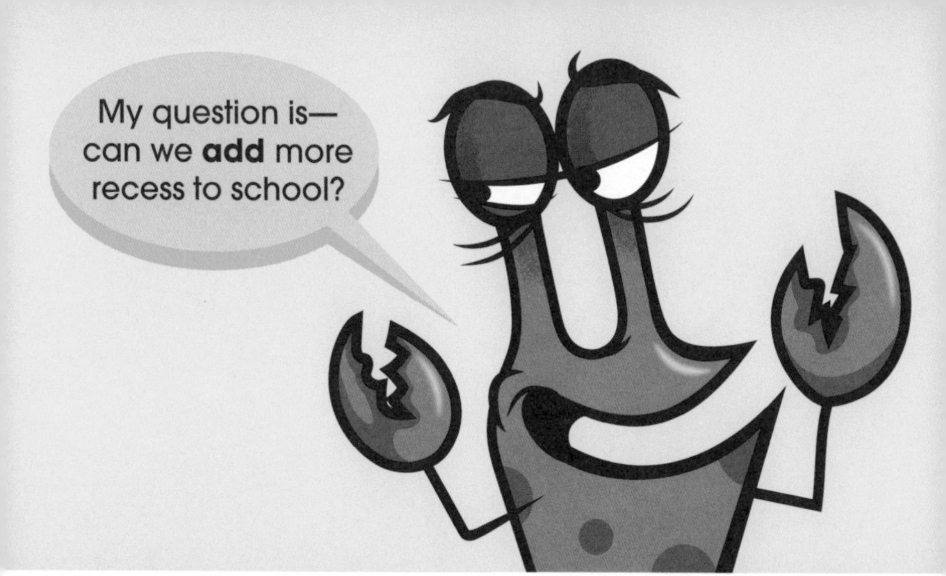
My question is—
can we **add** more
recess to school?

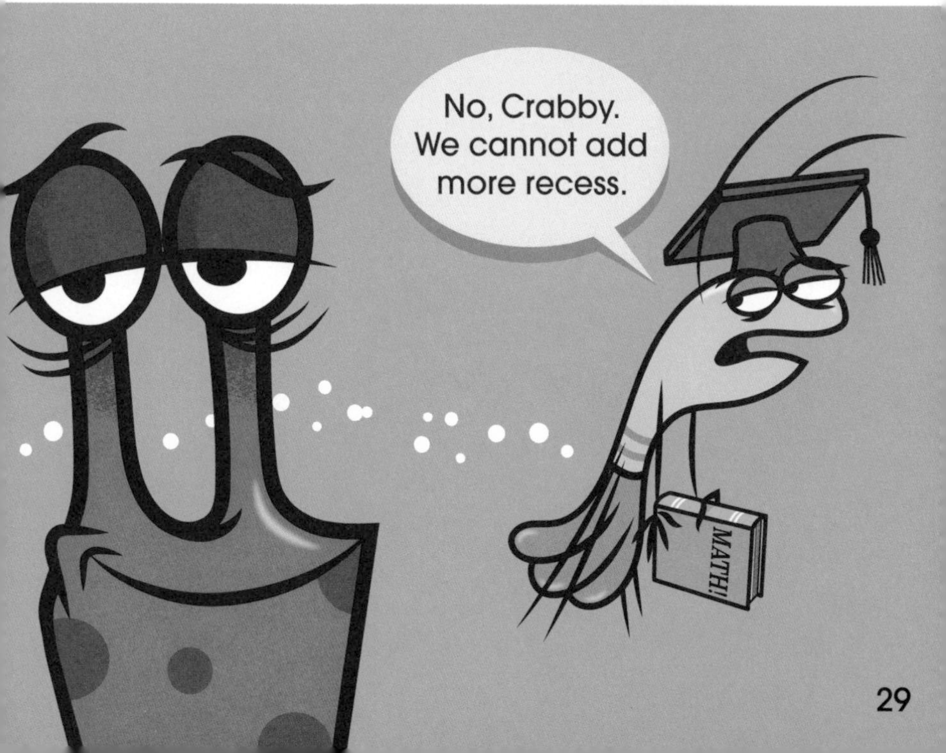
No, Crabby.
We cannot add
more recess.
MATH!

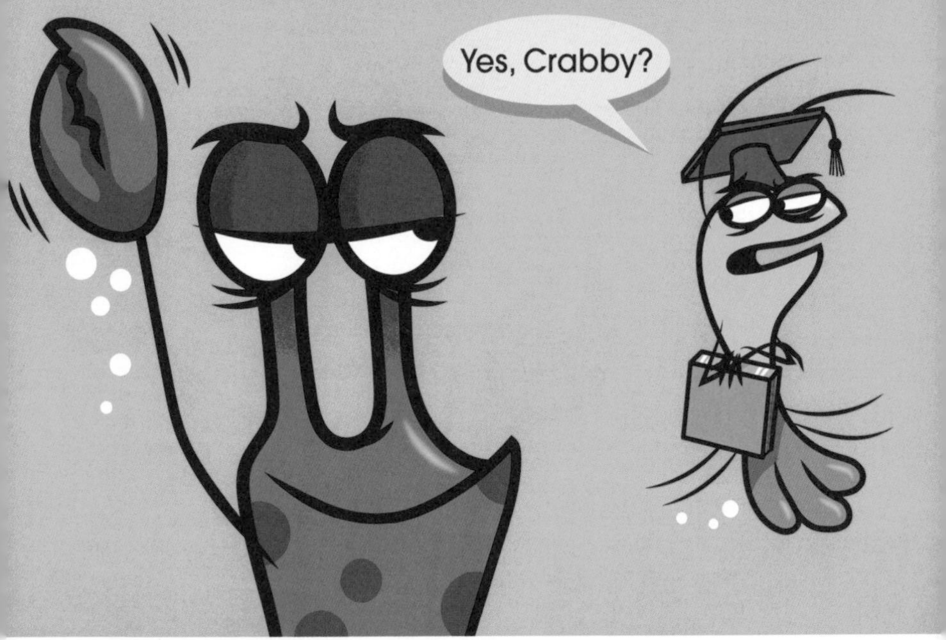
Yes, Crabby?

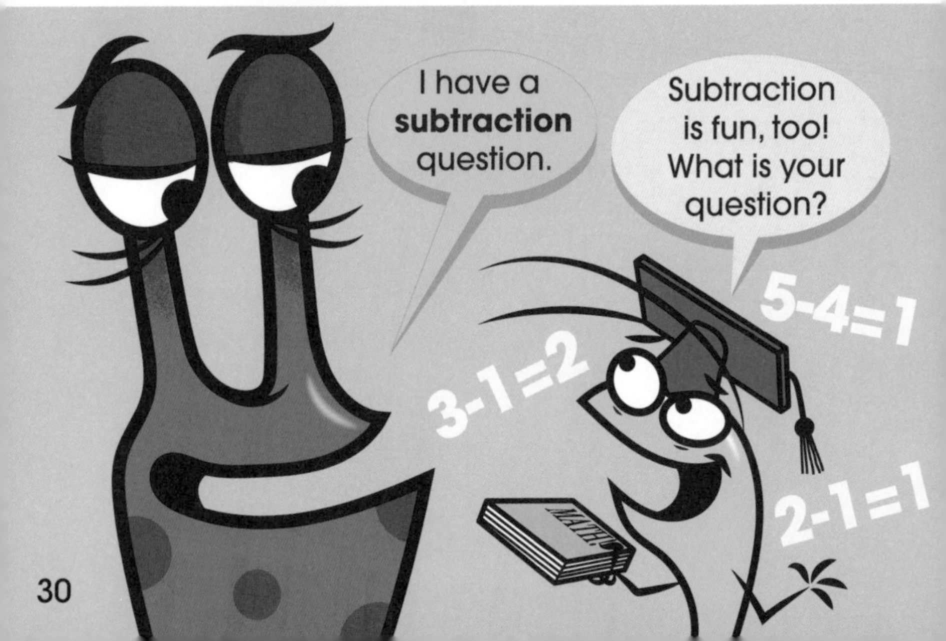
I have a **subtraction** question.
Subtraction is fun, too! What is your question?
5-4=1
3-1=2
2-1=1
MATH

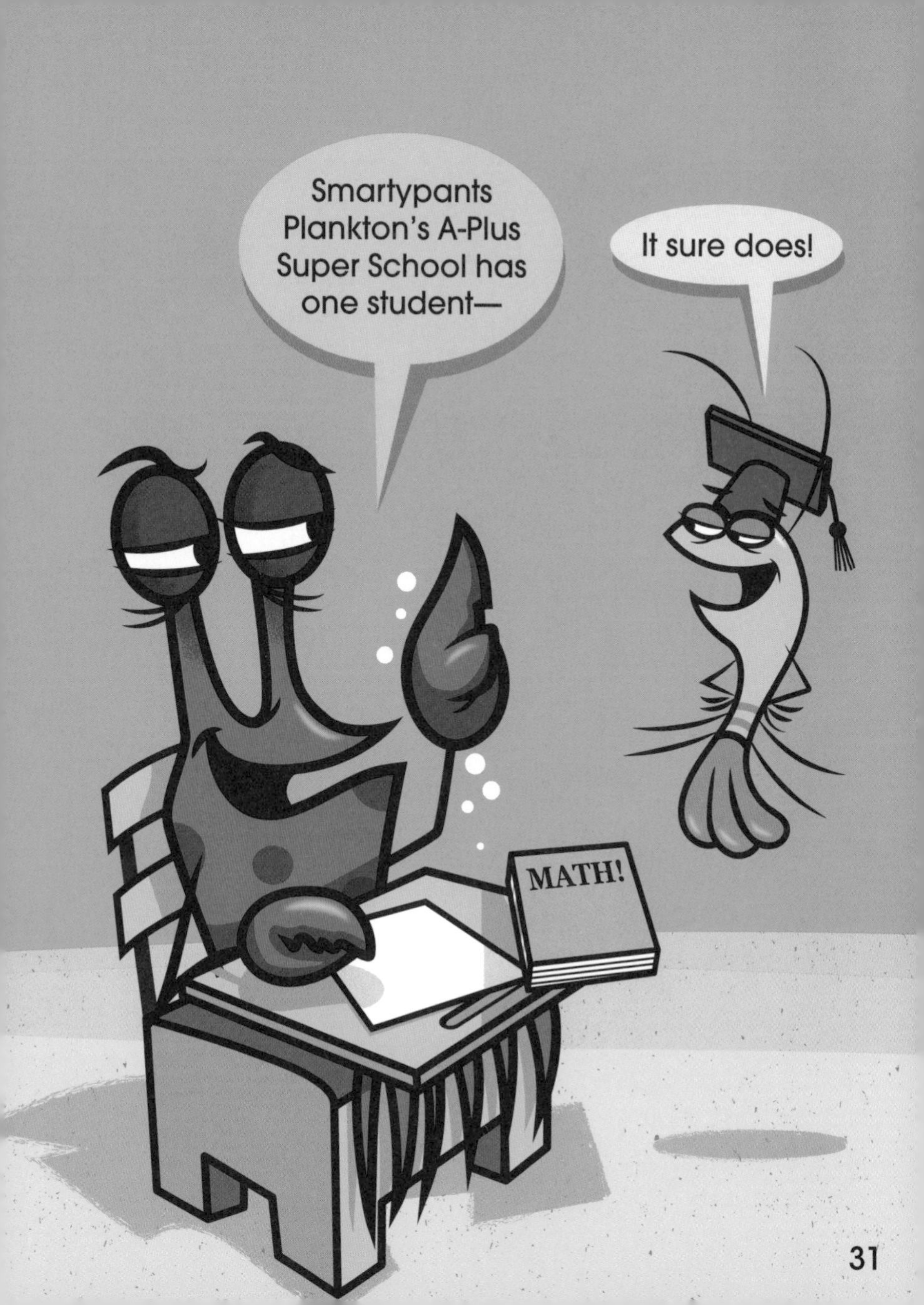
Smartypants Plankton's A-Plus Super School has one student—
It sure does!
MATH!

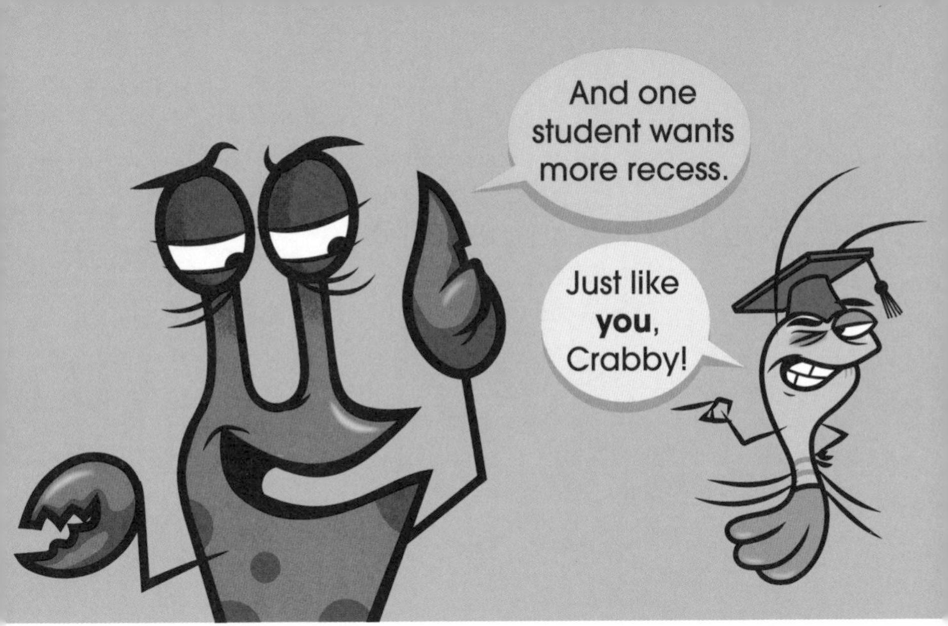
And one student wants more recess.
Just like **you**, Crabby!

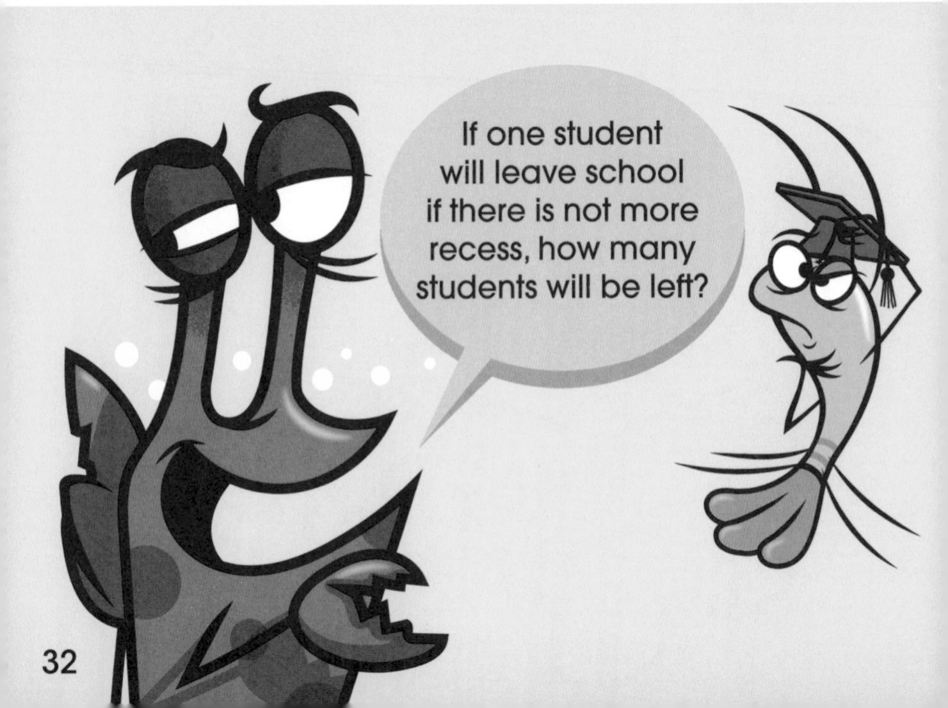
If one student will leave school if there is not more recess, how many students will be left?

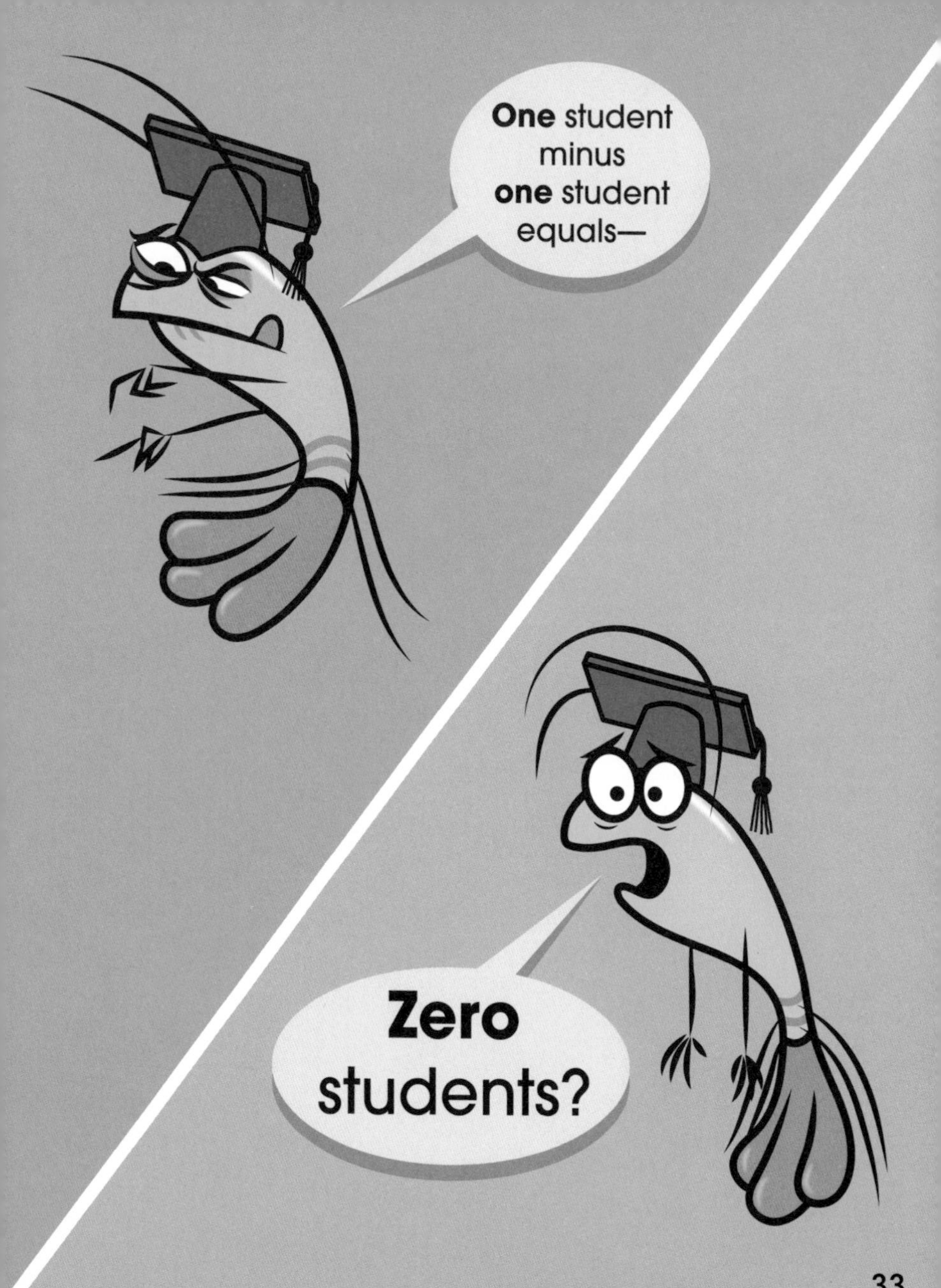
One student minus **one** student equals—
Zero students?

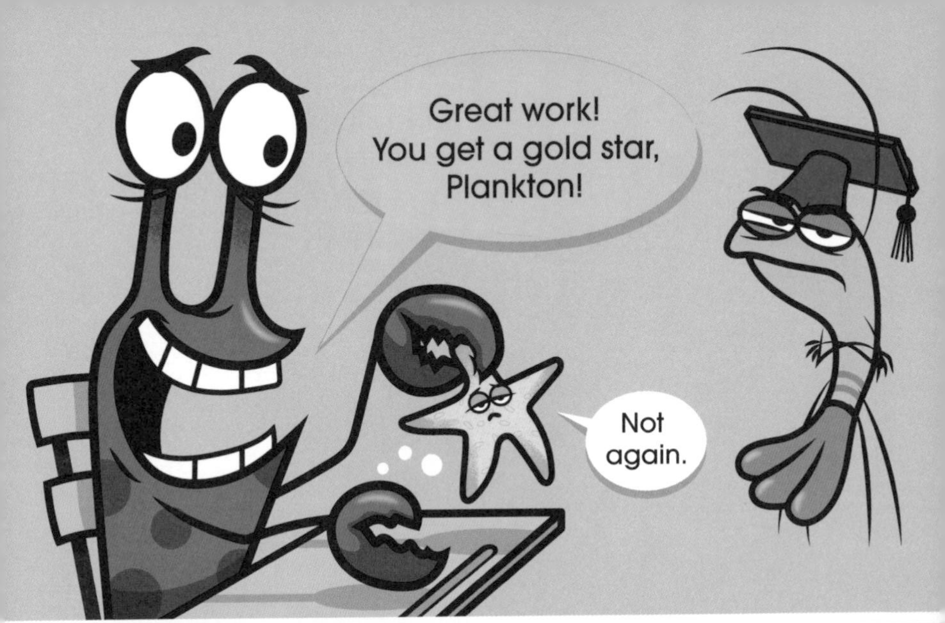
Great work! You get a gold star, Plankton!
Not again.

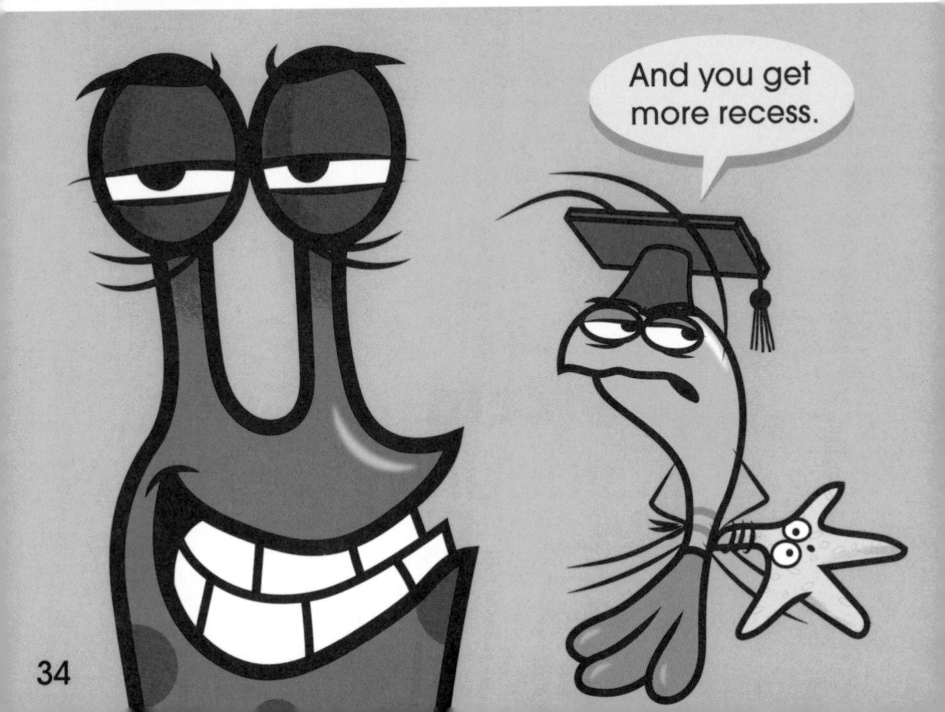
And you get more recess.

THE RULES

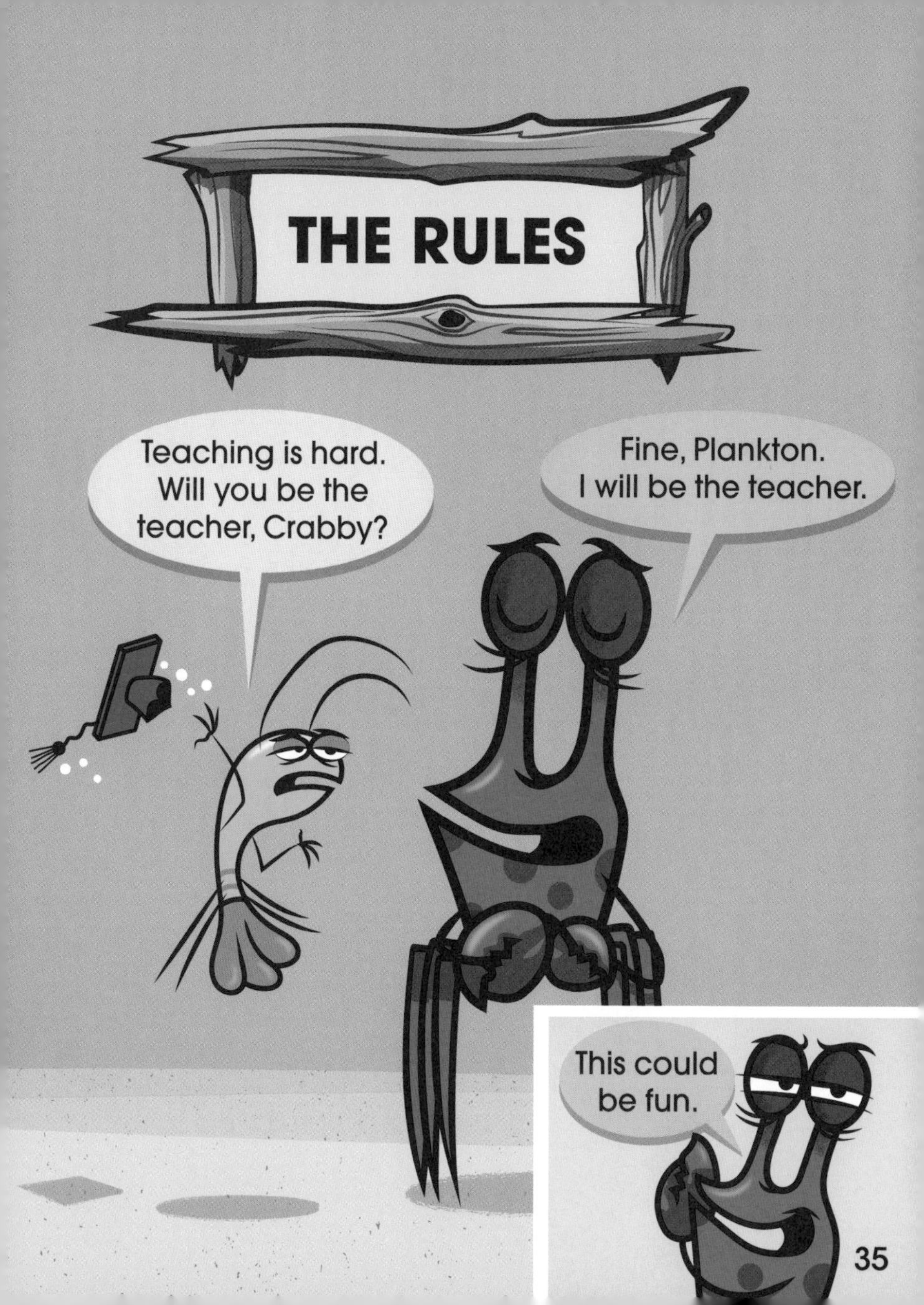
Teaching is hard. Will you be the teacher, Crabby?
Fine, Plankton. I will be the teacher.
This could be fun.

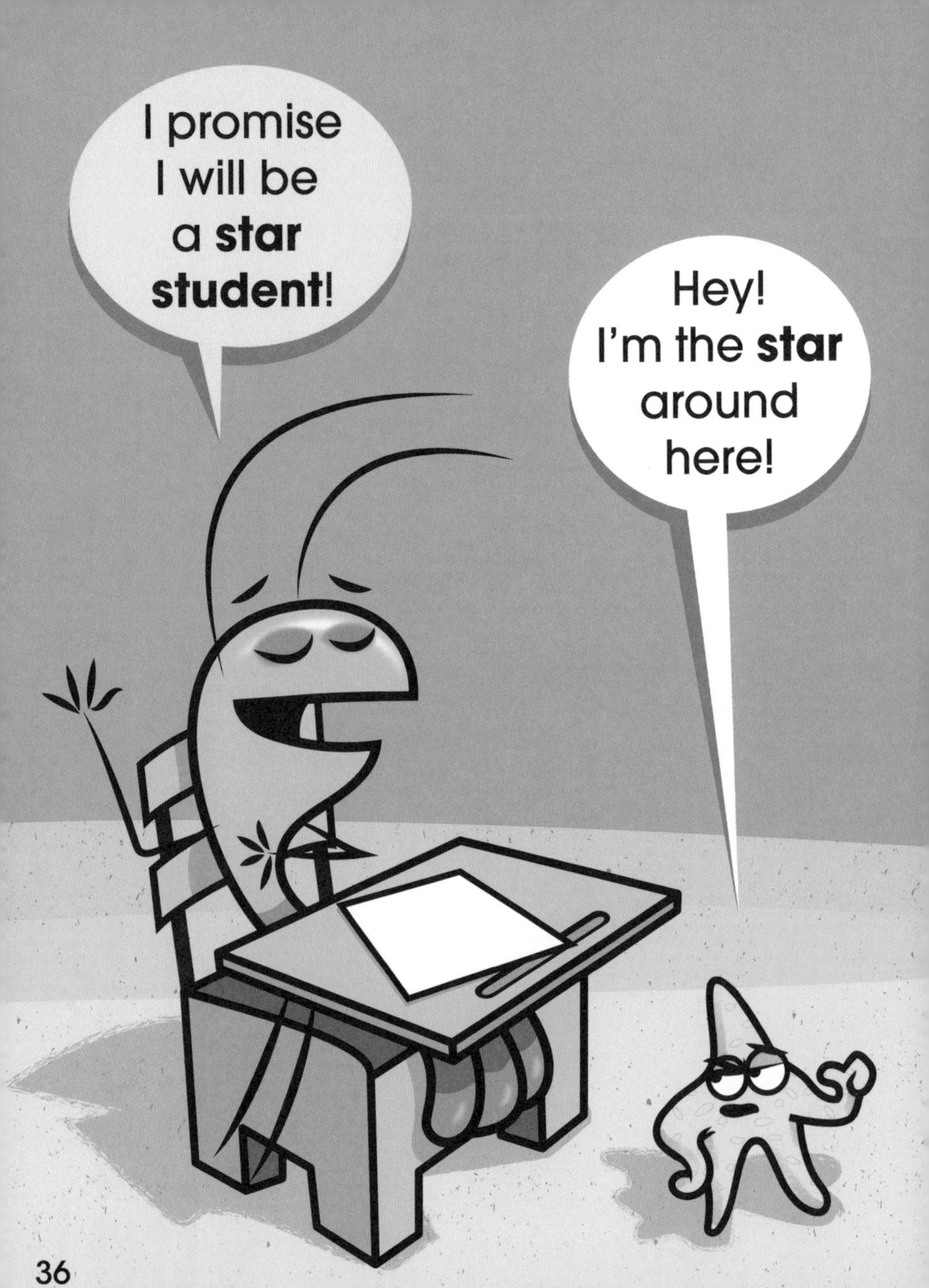
I promise I will be a **star** **student**!
Hey! I'm the **star** around here!

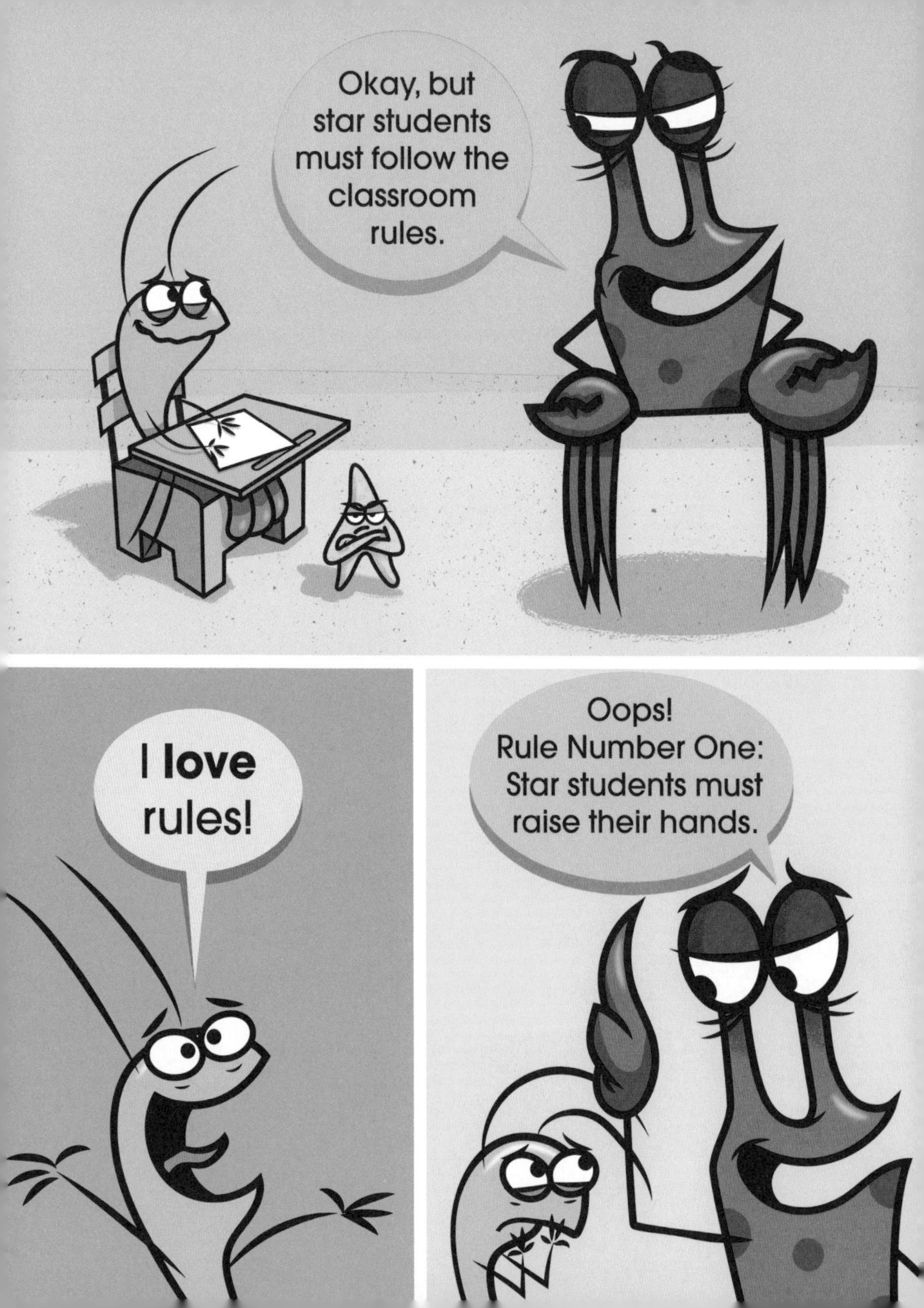
Okay, but star students must follow the classroom rules.
I **love** rules!
Oops! Rule Number One: Star students must raise their hands.

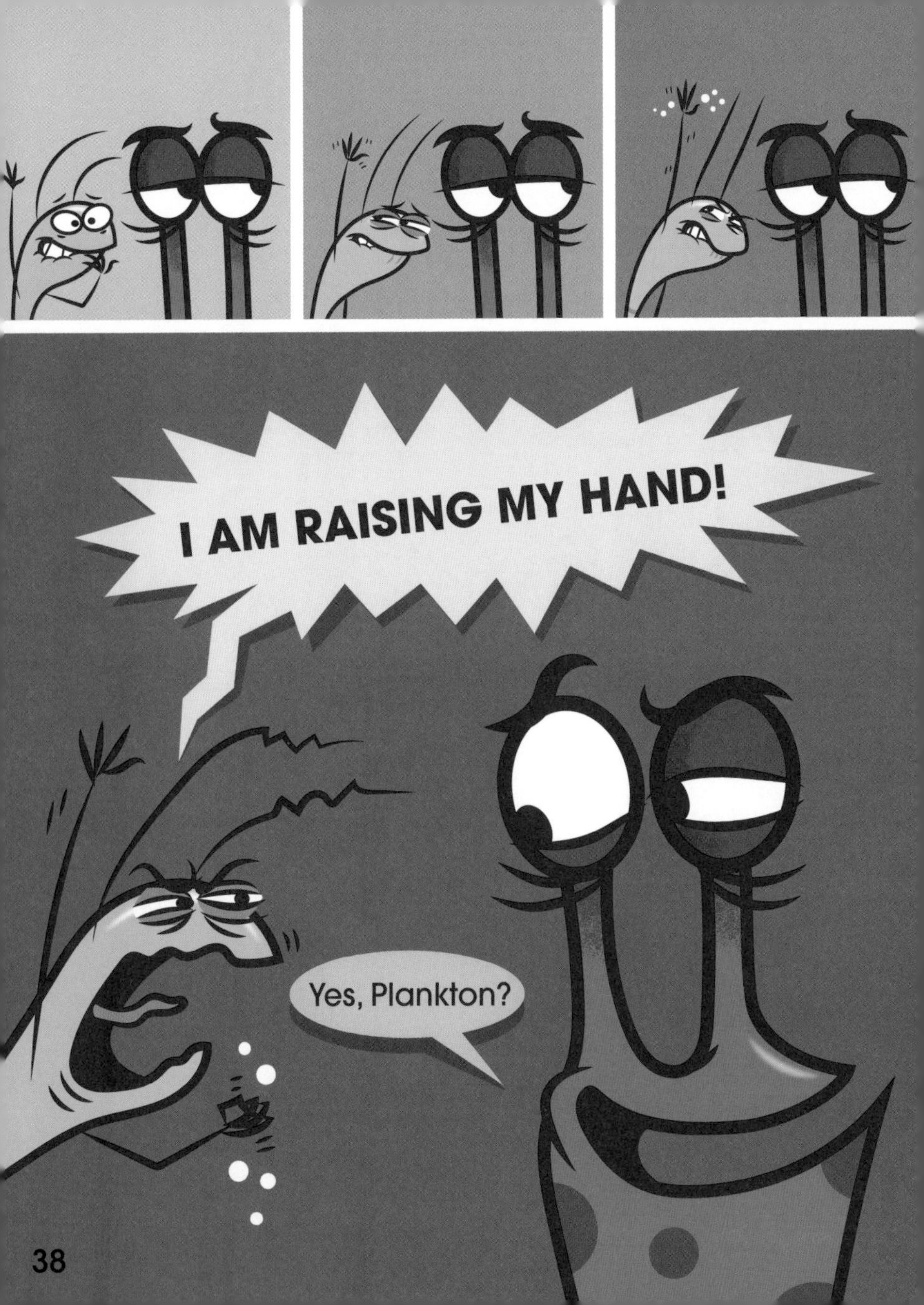
I AM RAISING MY HAND!
Yes, Plankton?

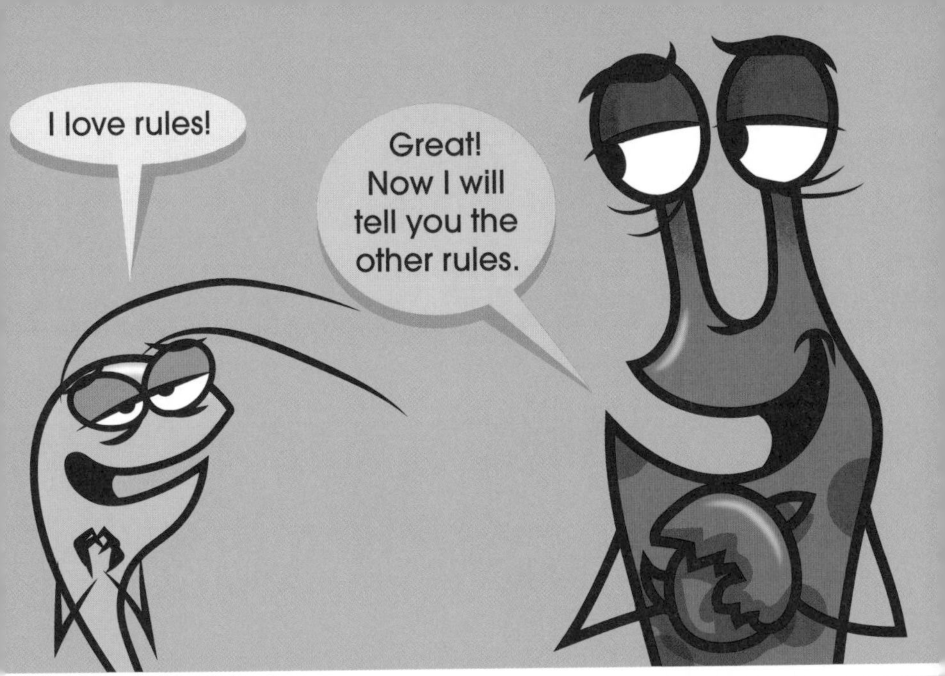
I love rules!
Great! Now I will tell you the other rules.

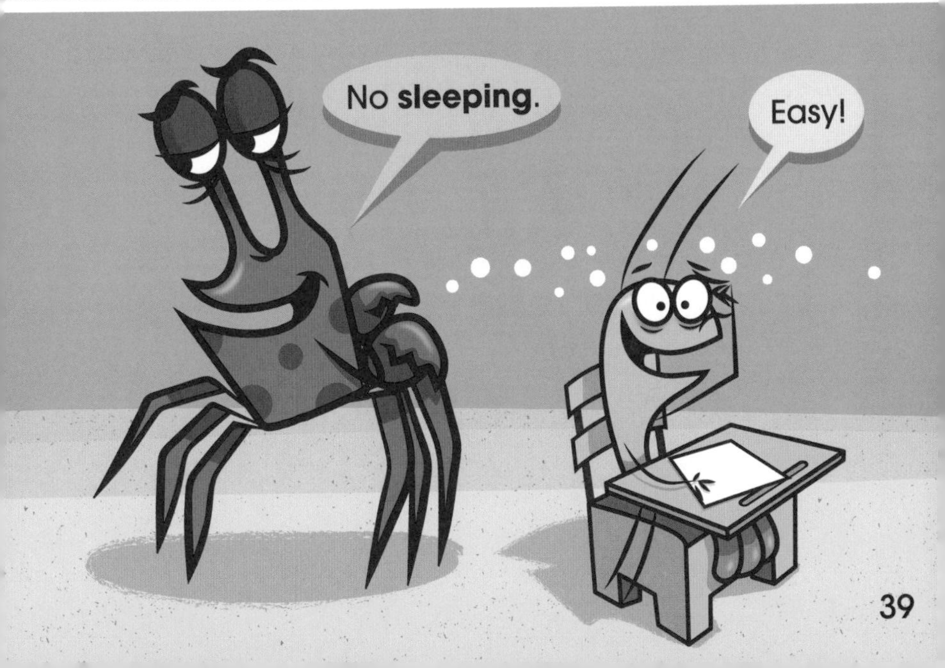
No **sleeping**.
Easy!

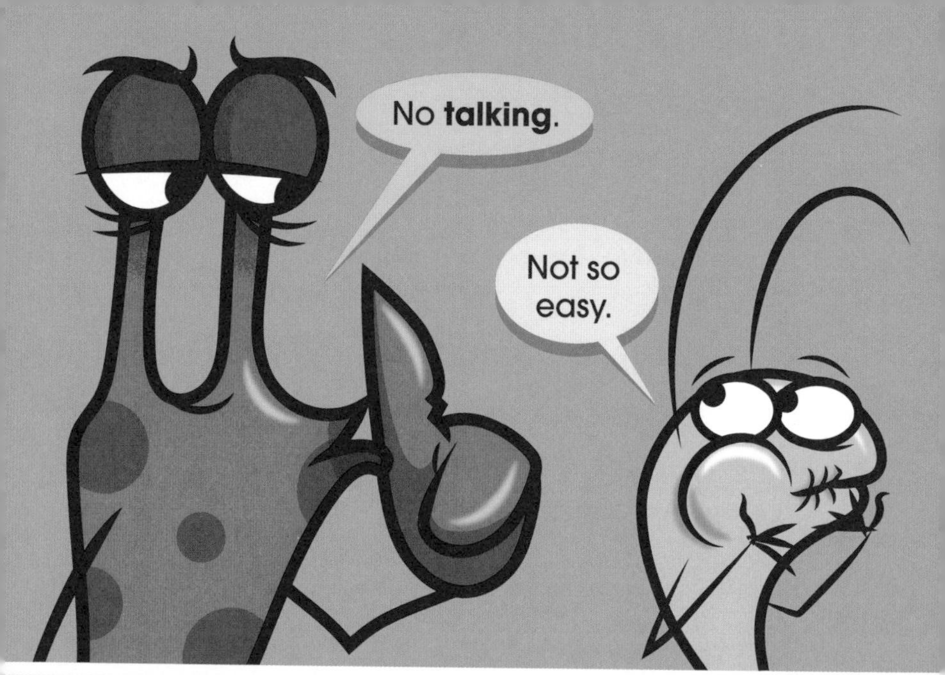
No **talking**.
Not so easy.

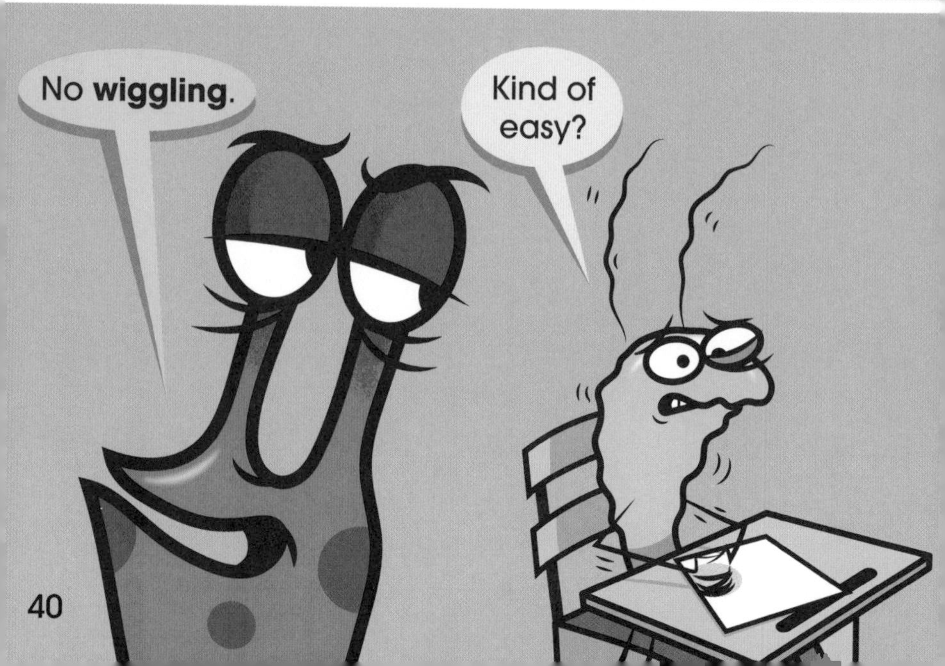
No **wiggling**.
Kind of easy?

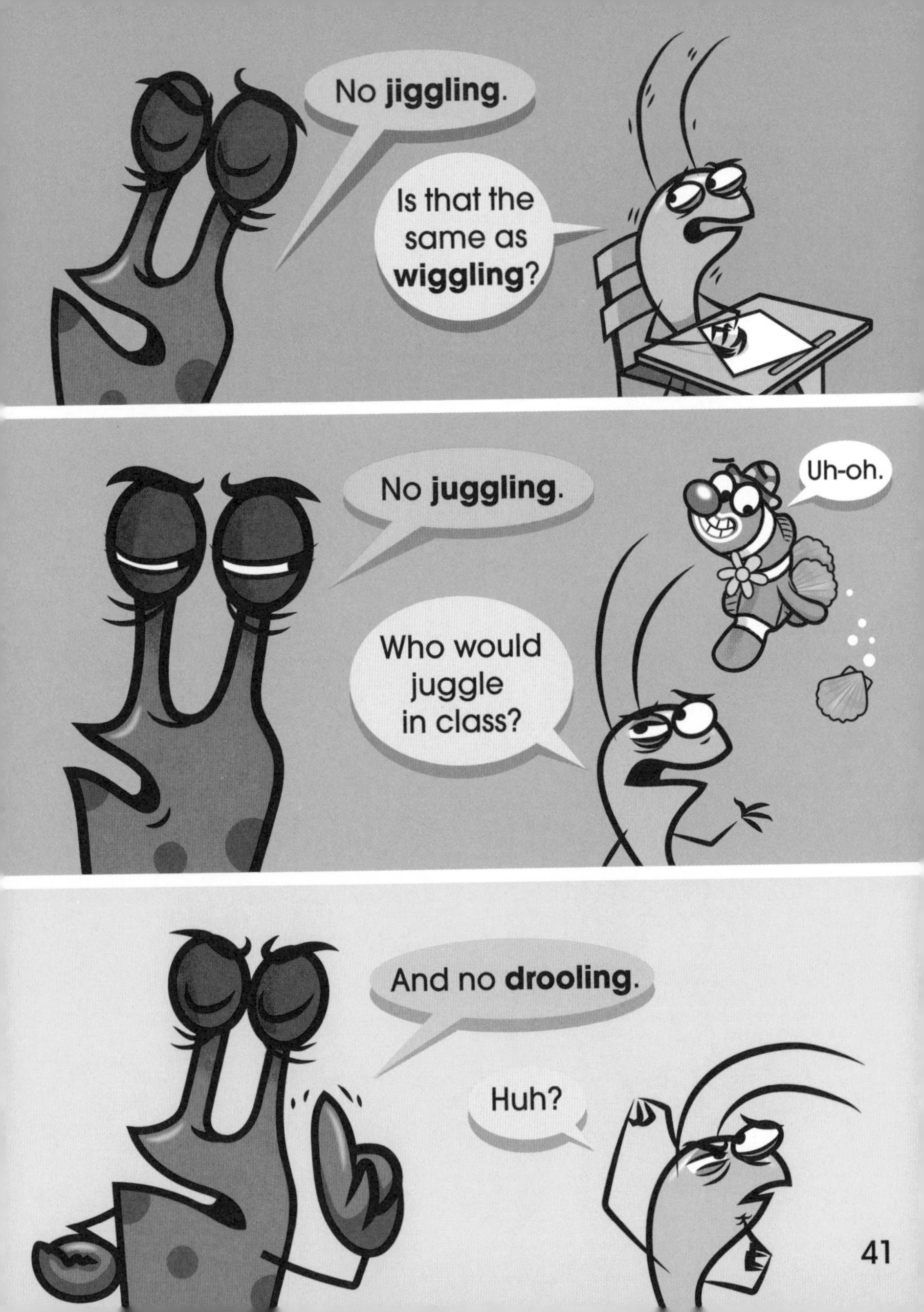
No **jiggling**.
Is that the same as **wiggling**?
No **juggling**.
Uh-oh.
Who would juggle in class?
And no **drooling**.
Huh?

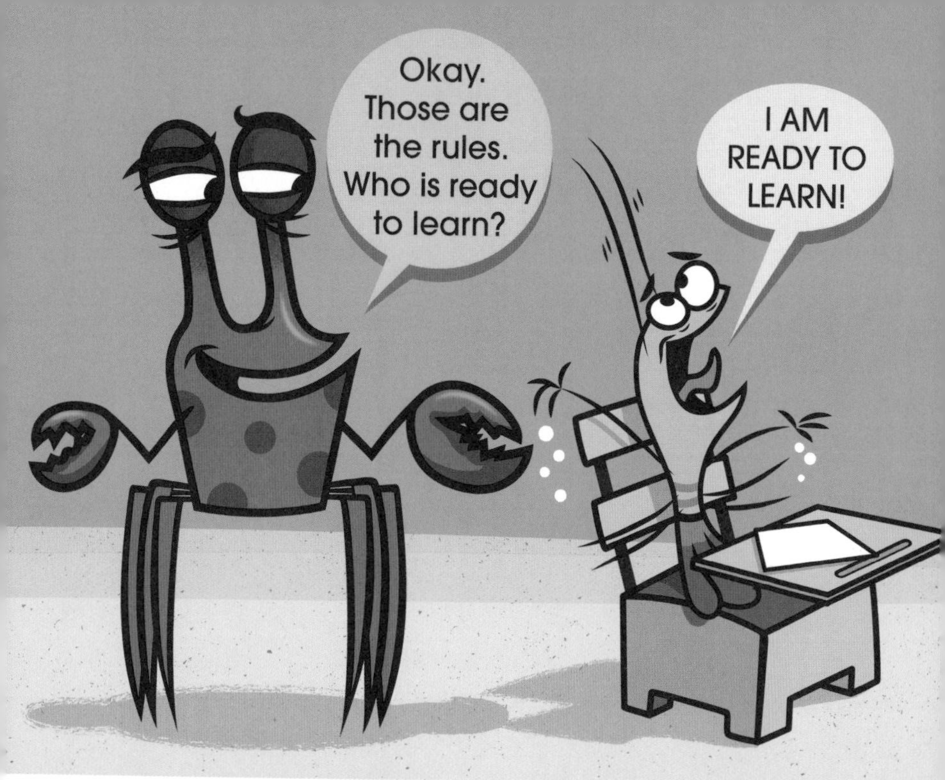
Okay. Those are the rules. Who is ready to learn?
I AM READY TO LEARN!

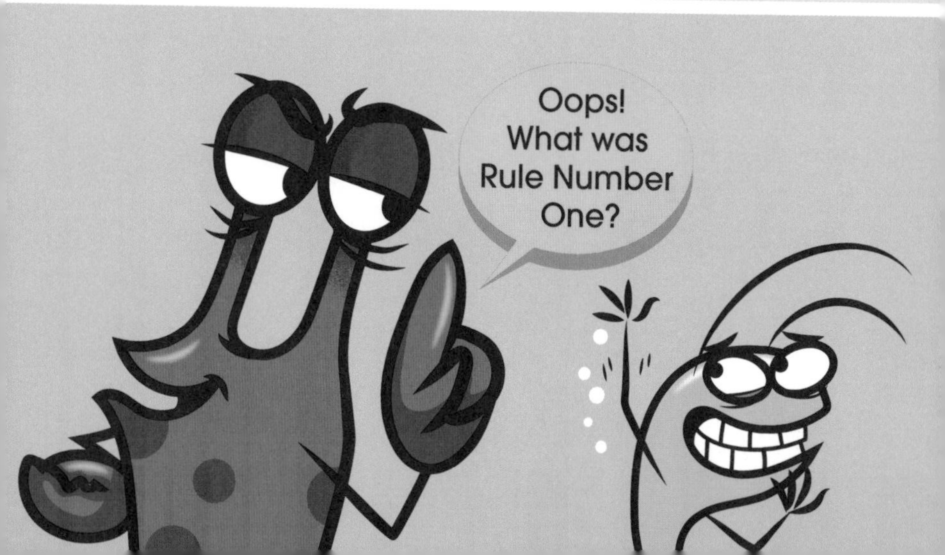
Oops! What was Rule Number One?

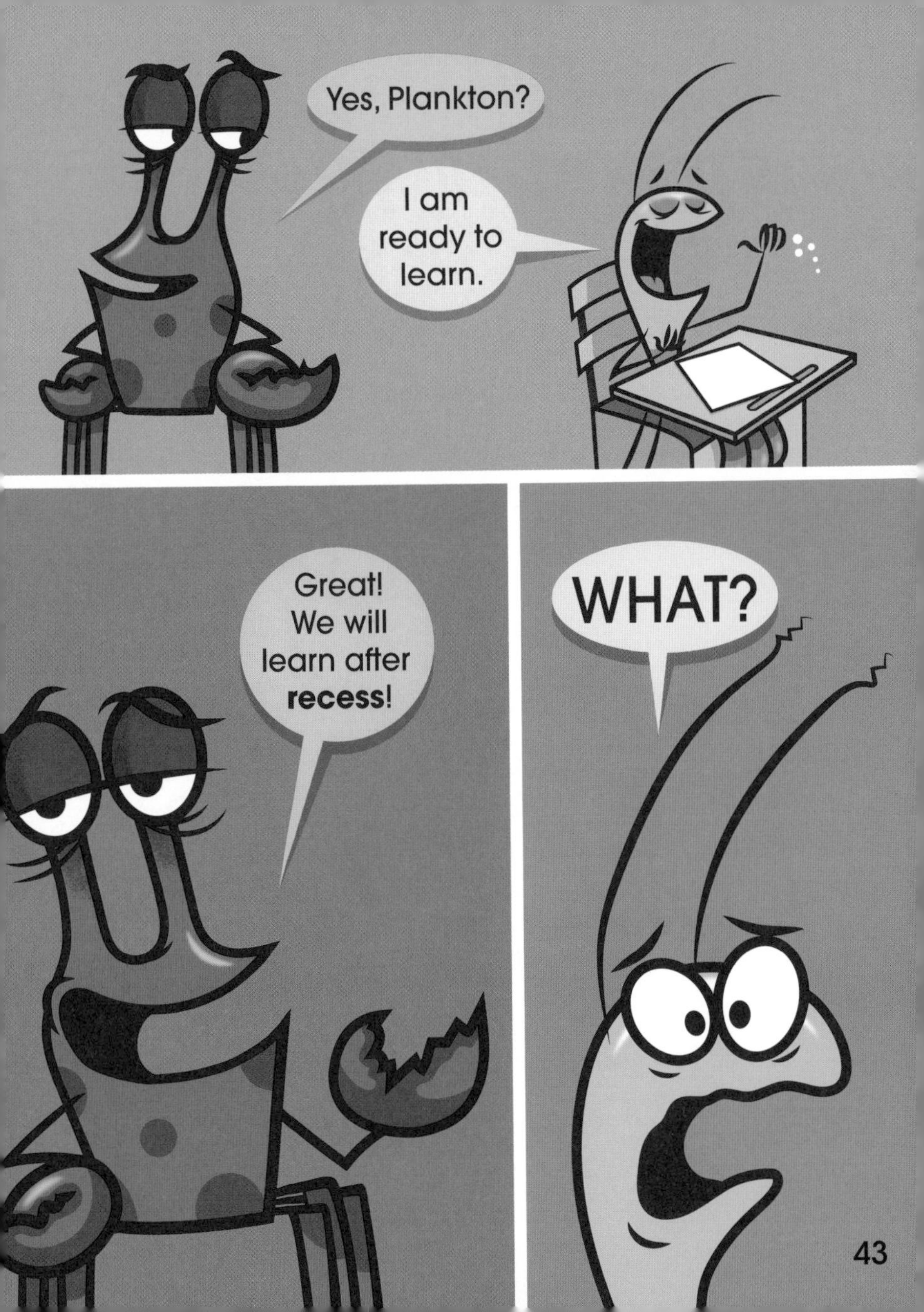
Yes, Plankton?
I am ready to learn.
Great! We will learn after **recess**!
WHAT?

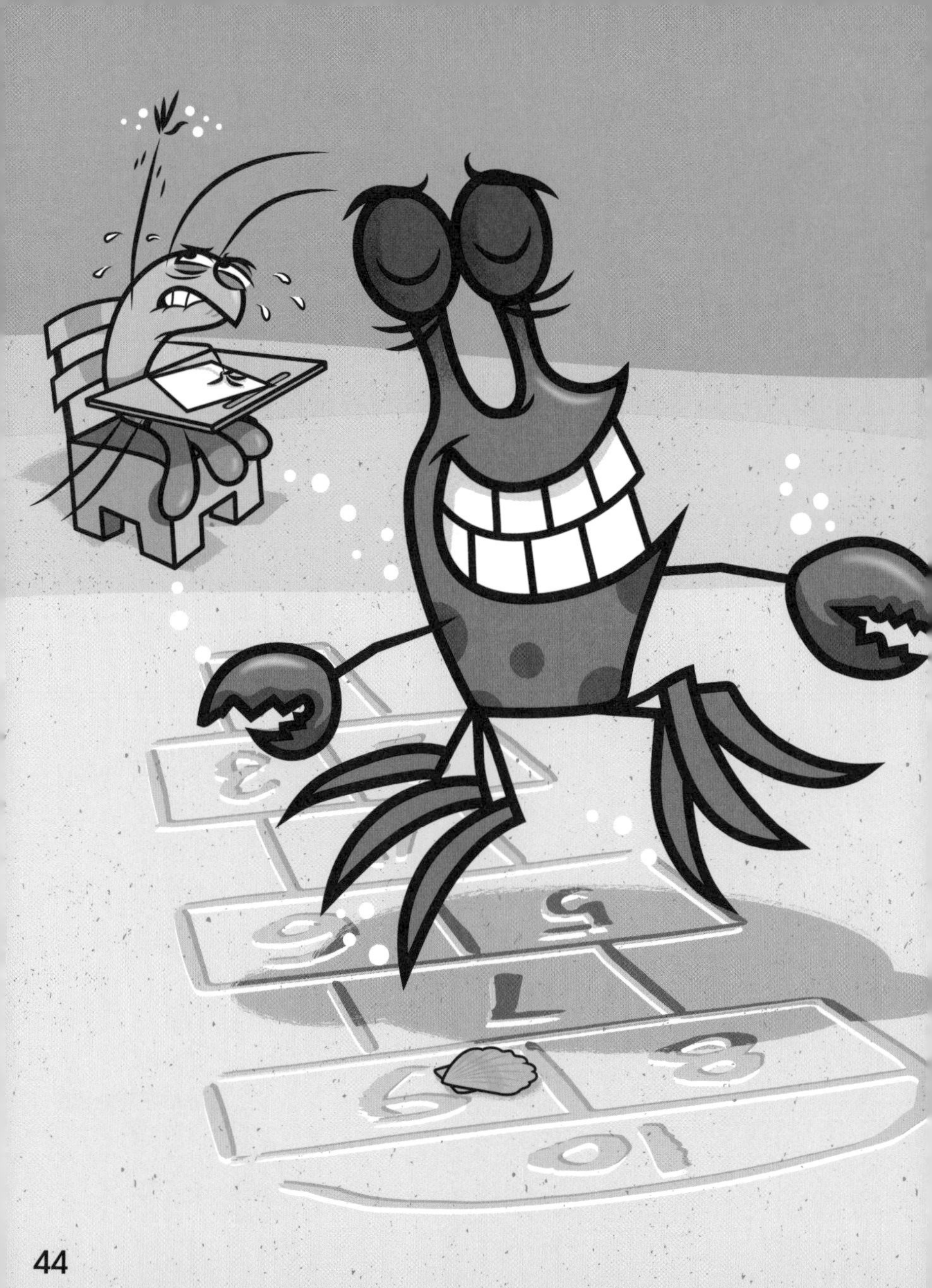

About the Author

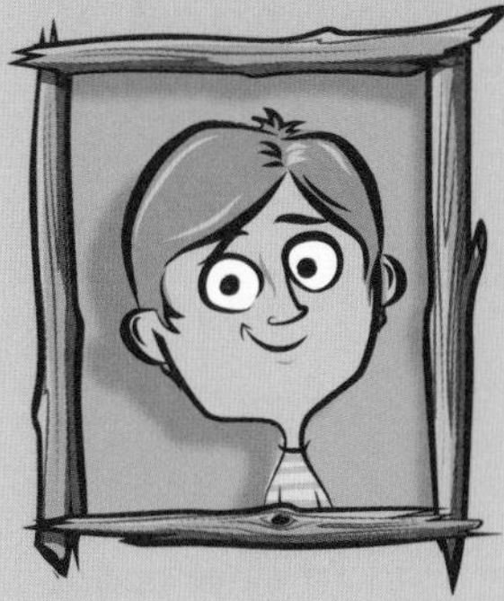

Jonathan Fenske lives in South Carolina with his family. He was born in Florida near the ocean, so he knows all about life at the beach! His favorite part of school was definitely recess!

Jonathan is the author and illustrator of several children's books including **Barnacle Is Bored**, **Plankton Is Pushy** (a Junior Library Guild selection), and **After Squidnight**. His early reader **A Pig, a Fox, and a Box** was a Theodor Seuss Geisel Honor Book.

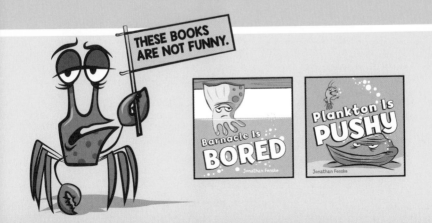

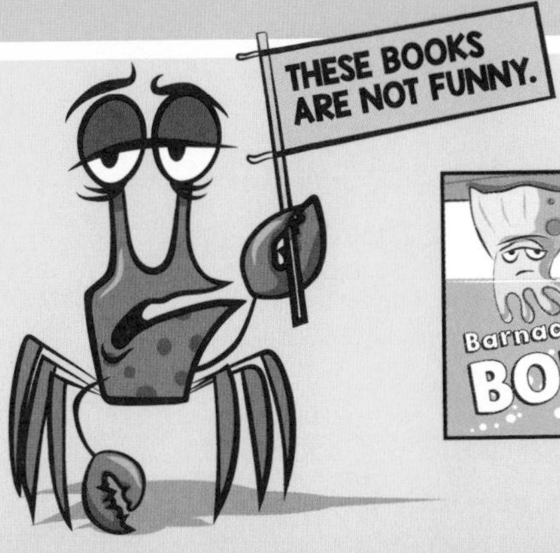
THESE BOOKS ARE NOT FUNNY.

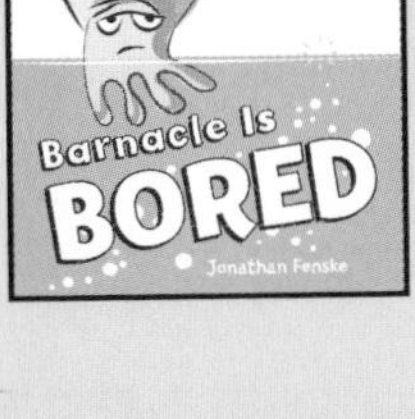
Barnacle Is
BORED
Jonathan Fenske

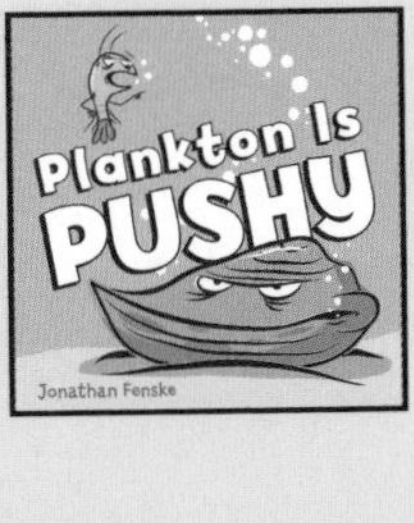
Plankton Is
PUSHY
Jonathan Fenske

YOU CAN DRAW FISHY!

I love school!

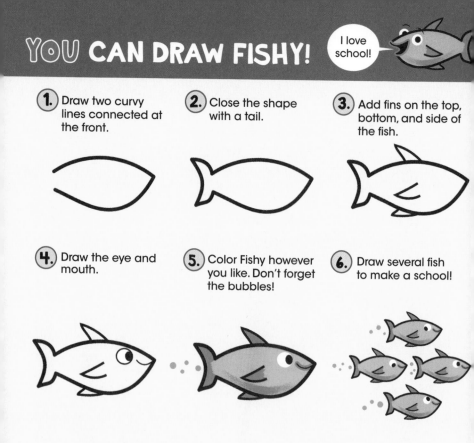

1. Draw two curvy lines connected at the front.

2. Close the shape with a tail.

3. Add fins on the top, bottom, and side of the fish.

4. Draw the eye and mouth.

5. Color Fishy however you like. Don't forget the bubbles!

6. Draw several fish to make a school!

WHAT'S YOUR STORY?

Plankton and Crabby are playing school!
What do you do during the school day?
Would you want Plankton or Crabby to be your teacher?
Write and draw your story!